The Voyeur

WORKS BY ALAIN ROBBE-GRILLET
PUBLISHED BY GROVE PRESS

The Erasers
The Voyeur
La Maison de Rendez-vous & Djinn
Two Novels: Jealousy & In the Labyrinth
Recollections of the Golden Triangle

Alain Robbe-Grillet

The Voyeur

Translated from the French by
RICHARD HOWARD

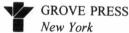 GROVE PRESS
New York

Published simultaneously in Canada
Printed in the United States of America

Library of Congress Catalog Card Number 58-9912

ISBN-10: 0-8021-3165-4
ISBN-13: 978-0-8021-3165-2

Grove Press
an imprint of Grove/Atlantic, Inc.
841 Broadway
New York, NY 10003
Distributed by Publishers Group West
www.groveatlantic.com

11 12 13 14 15   10 9 8 7

I

It was as if no one had heard.

The whistle blew again—a shrill, prolonged noise followed by three short blasts of ear-splitting violence: a violence without purpose that remained without effect. There was no more reaction—no further exclamation—than there had been at first; not one feature of one face had even trembled.

A motionless and parallel series of strained, almost anxious stares crossed—tried to cross—struggled against the narrowing space that still separated them from their goal. Every head was raised, one next to the other, in an identical attitude. A last puff of heavy, noiseless steam formed a great plume in the air above them, and vanished as soon as it had appeared.

Slightly to one side, behind the area in which the steam had just appeared, one passenger stood apart from the expectant group. The whistle had had no more effect on his withdrawal than on the passionate attention of his neighbors. Standing like them, his body and limbs rigid, he kept his eyes on the deck.

He had often heard the story before. When he was still a child—perhaps twenty-five or thirty years ago—he had

3

had a big cardboard box, an old shoebox, in which he collected pieces of string. Not any string, not scraps of inferior quality, worn, frayed bits that had been spoiled by overuse, not pieces too short to be good for anything.

This one would have been just right. It was a thin hemp cord in perfect condition, carefully rolled into a figure eight, with a few extra turns wound around the middle. It must be pretty long—a yard at least, perhaps two. Someone had probably dropped it by mistake after having rolled it up for future use—or else for a collection.

Mathias bent down to retrieve it. As he straightened up again he noticed, a few feet to the right, a little girl of seven or eight gravely staring at him, her eyes enormous and calm. He smiled hesitantly, but she did not bother to smile back, and it was only after several seconds that he saw her eyes shift toward the wad of string he was holding at the level of his chest. He was not disappointed by a closer look: it was a real find—not too shiny, firmly and regularly twisted, and evidently very strong.

For a moment he thought he recognized it, as if it were something he had lost long ago. A similar cord once must have occupied an important place in his thoughts. Would it be with the others in the shoebox? His memory immediately edged away toward the indefinite light of a rainy landscape, in which a piece of string played no perceptible part.

He had only to put it in his pocket. But no sooner had he begun the gesture than he stopped, his arm half-bent, undecided, gazing at his hand. He saw that his nails were too long, which he already knew. He also noticed that in growing their shape had become exaggeratedly pointed; naturally he did not file them to look like that.

The child was still staring in his direction, but it was difficult to be sure she was looking at him and not at something behind him, or even at nothing at all; her eyes seemed almost too wide to be able to focus on a single object, unless it was one of enormous size. She must have been looking at the sea.

Mathias let his arm fall to his side. Suddenly the engines stopped. The vibration ceased at once, as well as the continuous rumbling sound that had accompanied the ship since its departure. All the passengers remained silent, motionless, pressed close together at the entrance to the already crowded corridor through which they would eventually leave the ship. Most of them, ready for the disembarkation for some time, held their luggage in their hands, and all were facing left, their eyes fixed on the top of the pier where about twenty people were standing in a compact group, equally silent and rigid, looking for a familiar face in the crowd on the little steamer. In each group the expressions were identical: strained, almost anxious, strangely petrified and uniform.

The ship moved ahead under its own momentum, and the only sound that could be heard was the rustling of water as it slid past the hull. A gray gull, flying from astern at a speed only slightly greater than that of the ship, passed slowly on the port side in front of the pier, gliding at the level of the bridge without the slightest movement of its wings, its head cocked, one eye fixed on the water below —one round, indifferent, inexpressive eye.

There was the sound of an electric bell. The engines started up again. The ship began to make a turn that brought it gradually closer to the pier. The coast rapidly extended along the other side: the squat lighthouse striped black and white, the half-ruined fort, the sluice gates of the tidal basin, the row of houses on the quay.

"She's on time today," said a voice. "Almost," someone corrected—perhaps it was the same voice.

Mathias looked at his watch. The crossing had lasted exactly three hours. The electric bell rang again; then once more, a few seconds later. A gray gull resembling the first one passed by in the same direction, following the same horizontal trajectory in the same deliberate way—wings motionless, head cocked, beak pointing downward, one eye fixed.

The ship didn't seem to be moving in any direction at all. But the noise of violently churning water could be heard astern. The pier, now quite close, towered several yards above the deck. The tide must have been out. The landing slip from which the ship would be boarded revealed the smoother surface of its lower section, darkened by the water and half-covered with greenish moss. On closer inspection, the stone rim drew almost imperceptibly closer.

The stone rim—an oblique, sharp edge formed by two intersecting perpendicular planes: the vertical embankment perpendicular to the quay and the ramp leading to the top of the pier—was continued along its upper side at the top of the pier by a horizontal line extending straight toward the quay.

The pier, which seemed longer than it actually was as an effect of perspective, extended from both sides of this base line in a cluster of parallels describing, with a precision accentuated even more sharply by the morning light, a series of elongated planes alternately horizontal and vertical: the crest of the massive parapet that protected the tidal basin from the open sea, the inner wall of the parapet, the jetty along the top of the pier, and the vertical embankment that plunged straight into the water of the harbor. The two vertical surfaces were in shadow, the other two brilliantly lit by the sun—the whole breadth of the parapet and all of the jetty save for one dark narrow strip: the shadow cast by the parapet. Theoretically, the reversed image of the entire group could be seen reflected in the harbor water, and, on the surface, still within the same play of parallels, the shadow cast by the vertical embankment extending straight toward the quay.

At the end of the jetty the structure grew more elaborate; the pier divided into two parts: on the parapet side, a narrow passageway leading to a beacon light, and on the left the landing slip sloping down into the water. It was this latter inclined rectangle, seen obliquely, that attracted notice; slashed diagonally by the shadow of the embankment it skirted, it showed up as one dark triangle and one bright. All other surfaces were blurred. The water in the harbor was not calm enough for the reflection of the pier to be distinguished. Similarly the shadow of the pier appeared only as a vague strip constantly broken by surface undulations. The shadow of the parapet on the jetty tended to blend into the vertical surface which cast it. Jetty and parapet alike were still encumbered with drying fish, empty crates, large wicker baskets—crayfish and lobster traps, oyster hampers, crab snares. The crowd gathered for the ship's arrival circulated with some difficulty among the various piles of objects.

The ship itself floated so low on the ebb tide that it became impossible to see anything from its deck save the vertical embankment extending straight toward the quay and interrupted at its other end, just in front of the beacon, by the oblique landing slip—its lower section smoother, darkened by the water, and half-covered with greenish moss—still the same distance from the deck, as if all movement were at an end.

Nevertheless, on closer inspection the stone rim drew almost imperceptibly nearer.

The morning sun, slightly overcast as usual, indicated shadows faintly, yet sufficiently to divide the slope into two

symmetrical parts, one darker, one brighter, slanting a sharp
point of light toward the bottom where the water rose along
the slope, lapping between the strands of seaweed.

The movement bringing the little steamer nearer the
triangle of stone that thus emerged from the darkness was
itself an oblique one, and so deliberate as to be constantly
approaching absolute immobility.

Measured and even, despite slight variations of amplitude
and rhythm perceptible to the eye but scarcely exceeding
six inches and two or three seconds, the sea rose and fell
in the sheltered angle formed by the landing slip. On the
lower section of this inclined plane the water alternately
revealed and submerged great clumps of green seaweed.
From time to time, at what were doubtless regular intervals
—though probably of a more complex frequency—a powerful
wash of water broke this rocking rhythm and the two masses
of liquid, rushing against each other, collided with a slapping sound and spattered some drops of foam a little higher
up against the embankment.

The ship's side—now parallel to the embankment—continued to advance; the channel between must have narrowed
little by little as that movement extended the length of the
pier. Mathias tried to find a point of reference. In the angle
of the landing slip the water rose and fell against the brown
stone embankment. This far out from shore none of the
wreckage covering most harbor floors was visible from the
surface. The seaweed that grew at the bottom of the landing
slip, rising and falling again and again with the wash of
water, was as fresh and glossy as the kind found only at
great depths; it was never exposed to the air for very long
at a time. As each little wave rolled in, it lifted the free
ends of the clumps of seaweed, drew them down immediately afterward, and finally abandoned them once again,
limp and outstretched on the streaming stones, trailing

masses of tangled ribbon down the slope. From time to time a more powerful wash of water flooded the landing slip a little higher, leaving, as it flowed back, a shiny puddle in a hollow of the pavement that reflected the sky for a few seconds before it quickly disappeared between the stones.

Mathias decided on a mark shaped like a figure eight, cut clearly enough in the steep, recessed embankment to make a good point of reference. The mark was exactly opposite him, that is, ten or fifteen feet to the left of the point where the landing slip emerged from the pier. A sudden rise in the water level caused it to disappear. When, after forcing himself to keep his eyes in the same place for several seconds, he saw it again, he was not quite sure he was looking at the same mark—other irregularities in the stone looked just as much like—or unlike—the two little coupled circles whose shape he still remembered.

Something fell, thrown from the top of the pier, landing on the surface of the water—a piece of paper the color of a pack of cigarettes. The water rose in the sheltered angle of the landing slip, colliding with the backwash from its sloping surface. The periodic shock of this collision occurred just where the ball of blue paper was floating, and it was engulfed with a slapping sound; some drops of foam were spattered against the embankment, just as a more powerful wash of water again submerged the strands of seaweed and reached as far as the hollow in the pavement.

The water fell back at once; the limp seaweed remained outstretched on the wet rocks, trailing long strands down the slope. In the bright triangle, the little puddle reflected the sky.

Before it had time to disappear between the stones, this reflection was suddenly darkened, as if by the shadow of some great bird. Mathias raised his eyes. Flying from astern, the gray gull imperturbably described again, with the same deliberation, its horizontal trajectory—wings motionless and outspread in a double arc between the slightly drooping tips, head cocked to the right, one round eye fixed on the water—or the ship—or nothing at all.

According to their respective positions, it could not have been this gull's shadow that had just passed over the little puddle.

In the bright triangle the hollow of the pavement was dry. At the lower edge of the landing slip a rising wash of water had turned the seaweed so that it spread upward. Ten or fifteen feet to the left Mathias noticed the mark in the shape of a figure eight.

It was an eight on its side: two coupled circles of the same size, a little less than six inches in diameter. At the point of tangency appeared a reddish excrescence that looked like the rust-corroded pivot of an old iron ring. The circles on either side might have been worn gradually into the stone by a ring fastened vertically into the embankment' by the pivot and swinging freely to the right or left in the wash of the ebb tide. Such a ring had doubtless been used for mooring boats at the pier ahead of the landing slip.

But the ring had been set so low in the embankment that it must have been underwater most of the time—sometimes several yards beneath the surface. Furthermore, its modest size scarcely seemed adequate to the thickness of the ropes ordinarily used for mooring even the smallest fishing boats. The only rope that could have passed through such a ring would have to be a thin, strong cord. Mathias turned his eyes ninety degrees toward the crowd of passengers, then lowered them to the deck. He had often heard the story before. It was on a rainy day; he had been left alone in the house; instead of doing the next day's arithmetic home-work he had spent all afternoon sitting at the back window, drawing a sea gull that had perched on one of the fence posts at the end of the garden.

It had been a rainy day—to all appearances a rainy day like the rest. He was sitting at the table wedged into the window recess, facing the window, two big books under the chair so he could work comfortably. The room must have been very dark; the table top reflected only enough light from outside to make the waxed oak gleam—very faintly. The notebook's white paper constituted the only bright thing in the room, along with the child's face, and perhaps his hands as well. He was sitting on a chair on top of two dictionaries—had been there for hours, probably. He had almost finished his drawing.

The room was very dark. Outside it was raining. The big gull remained motionless on its perch. He had not seen it land there. He did not know how long it had been where it was. Usually they did not come so near the house, not even in the worst weather, although between the garden and the sea there was no more than three hundred yards of open ground rolling toward an indentation in the coast, bounded on the left by the beginning of the cliff. The garden here was nothing but a piece of moorland planted with potatoes every year and fenced off with barbed-wire fastened to wooden posts to keep out the sheep. The unwieldy size of these posts indicated that originally they had not been intended for such use. The fence post at the end of the central path was even thicker than the rest, in spite of the slenderness of the lattice-gate it supported; it was a cylindrical post, a pine log roughly trimmed, and its almost flat top, a yard and a half above the ground, formed an ideal perch for the gull. The bird's head was turned toward the fence, in profile, one eye looking at the sea, the other at the house.

Between the fence and the house the garden, at this time of year, consisted of little more than a few late weeds piercing the carpet of dead vegetation that had been rotting in the rain for several days.

The weather was very calm, without a breath of wind. The continuous light rain may have blurred the horizon, but did not obstruct the view for shorter distances. On the contrary, it was as if in this new-washed air the objects near at hand profited from an additional luster—especially when they were light-colored to begin with, like the gull. He had copied not only the contours of its body, the folded gray wing, the single foot (which completely concealed the other one), and the white head with its round eye, but also the wavy line dividing the two parts of its curved, pointed bill, the pattern of the feathers on its tail and along the edges of its wing, and even the overlapping scales down the length of its leg.

He was drawing on very smooth paper with a hard-lead pencil. Although scarcely pressing down at all, in order not to leave an impression on the next pages in the notebook, he obtained a clear, black line; he had taken such care to reproduce his model faithfully that there was no need to erase. His head bent over his work, his forearms resting on the oak table, he began to feel tired from sitting so long in one position, his legs dangling over the edge of the hard, uncomfortable chair. But he did not want to move.

Behind him the whole house was empty and black. Except when the morning sun brightened them, the front rooms, facing the road, were even darker than the others. Yet this room, where he had settled down to work, was lighted by only one small, square window deeply recessed in the wall; the carpet was very dark, the high, heavy, dark-stained furniture crowded close together. There were at least three heavy wardrobe-cupboards, two of them side by side oppo-

site the door opening onto the hallway. On a lower shelf
of the third one, in the right-hand corner, was the shoebox
in which he kept his string collection.

The water level rose and fell in the sheltered angle at
the bottom of the landing slip. The ball of blue paper,
quickly saturated, had half unfolded and was floating between two waves a few inches below the surface. It was
easier to tell now that it was the paper from a pack of
cigarettes. It rose and fell, following the movement of the
water, but always at the same point—neither closer to nor
farther away from the embankment, moving neither to the
right nor the left. Its position was easy for Mathias to
establish, for it was on a line with the mark shaped like a
figure eight.

The moment he became aware of this fact, he noticed,
about a yard away from the first mark and at the same
height, another design shaped like a figure eight—two circles
incised side by side, and between them the same reddish
excrescence that seemed to be the remains of a piece of
iron. There must have been two rings fixed into the embankment. The one nearer the landing slip immediately disappeared, submerged by a wave. Then the other one was
engulfed in its turn.

The water, falling back from the vertical embankment,
collided with the backwash from the inclined plane of the
landing slip; a little cone of liquid leaped toward the sky
with a slapping sound, and a few drops fell back around
it; then everything was as it had been before. Mathias
looked for the floating cigarette pack—it was impossible to
tell exactly where it would surface again. He is sitting at
the table wedged into the window recess, facing the window.

The window is almost square—a yard wide and hardly
any higher—four identical panes—with neither curtain nor
shade. It is raining. The sea is invisible, though quite near.

Although it is broad daylight, there is just enough light from outside to make the waxed table top gleam—very faintly. The rest of the room is very dark, for in spite of its rather large size it has only this one aperture, which furthermore happens to be located in a recess in the wall. A good half of the square, dark-stained oak table is wedged into the recess. On the table the white pages of the notebook, placed parallel to the edge, constitute the only bright thing in the room—not counting, above them, four slightly larger rectangles: the four panes of the window opening onto the fog that conceals the entire landscape.

He is sitting on a bulky chair that is on top of two dictionaries. He is drawing. He is drawing a big gray and white sea gull. The bird's head is facing toward the right, in profile. The wavy line dividing the two parts of its curved, pointed bill can be distinguished, as well as the pattern of the feathers on its tail and along the edge of its wing, and even the overlapping scales down the length of its leg. Yet it seems as if something is missing.

There was something missing from the drawing, although it was difficult to tell exactly what. Mathias decided that something was either not correctly drawn—or else missing altogether. Instead of the pencil, his right hand was holding the wad of cord he had just picked up from the deck. He looked at the group of passengers in front of him, as if he were hoping to find among them the object's owner coming toward him, smiling, to ask for its return. But no one paid any attention to him or to his discovery; they all continued to turn their backs. Slightly to one side, the little girl seemed to be forsaken. She was standing against one of the iron pillars that supported the deck above. Her hands were clasped behind the small of her back, her legs braced and slightly spread, her head leaning against the column; even in a position as rigid as this the child maintained something of her graceful attitude. Her face shone with the confident, yet conscious gentleness imagination attributes to obedient children. She had been in the same position ever since Mathias first noticed her presence; she was still looking in the same direction, toward where the sea had been and where now the vertical embankment of the pier rose above them—quite close by.

Mathias had just stuffed the cord into the pocket of his duffle coat. He caught sight of his empty right hand, its nails too long and too pointed. To give those five fingers something to do, he gripped them around the handle of the little suitcase he had been holding in his other hand. It was an ordinary enough suitcase, but its solid manufacture inspired confidence: it was made of a very hard, reddish-brown fiber, the corners reinforced with some material of a darker, almost chocolate color. The handle, fastened with two metal clasps, was made of a softer, imitation-leather material. The lock, the two hinges, and the three big rivets at each of the eight corners looked like copper, as did the clasps of the handle, but even slight wear had already revealed the real composition of the four rivets on the bottom: copper-plated babbit metal, which was obviously what the other twenty rivets were made of—and doubtless the rest of the fittings as well.

The inside was lined with printed cretonne, of which the pattern only superficially resembled those customarily used for materials of this type, even in women's or girls' luggage; instead of bouquets or sprays of flowers, the decorative motif consisted of tiny dolls, like those used on nursery curtains. But unless examined closely, it was not apparent that they were dolls: they looked more like bright-colored spots on the pale canvas—they might just as well have been bouquets of flowers. The suitcase contained an ordinary memorandum book, a few prospectuses, and eighty-nine wrist watches

mounted in rows of ten on nine rectangular strips of cardboard, one of which had an empty mounting.

Mathias had already made his first sale that same morning, before boarding the ship. Even though it had been a
watch from the cheapest row—one hundred fifteen crowns—
on which he realized the most slender profit, he decided to
consider this early start as a good omen. On this island,
where he had been born, after all, and where he was per-
sonally acquainted with many families—where, at least, in
spite of his bad memory for faces, he could make a harmless
pretense of renewing old friendships, thanks to the inquiries
he had made the day before—he had a good chance of selling most of his merchandise in a few hours. In spite of the
fact that he had to leave on the four o'clock boat, it was
even possible—or not materially impossible—to sell every
watch he had brought in the course of this one short day.
Furthermore, he was not even limited to the contents of his
suitcase: in the past he had occasionally taken orders for
articles which were paid for on delivery.

But counting only the ninety watches which were in his
luggage, the profit would be considerable: ten at a hundred
fifteen crowns, eleven hundred fifty, ten at one hundred
thirty, thirteen hundred, fourteen hundred fifty, ten at one
hundred fifty, four with a special wristband at five crowns
extra apiece. . . . To simplify matters Mathias decided on an
average price of two hundred crowns; the week before he
had calculated the exact amount that a similar batch was
worth, and two hundred crowns was a good approximation.
So he should total about eighteen thousand crowns. His
gross profit varied between twenty-six and thirty-eight per
cent; figuring on an average of thirty per cent—three times
eight, twenty-four, three times one, three, three and two,
five—it came to more than five thousand crowns, that is, the
gross profit was actually worth a whole week's work—even

during a good week—in his usual territory. As for personal expenses, there would be only the sixty crowns for the round-trip boat fare, which was practically negligible.

It had taken hopes of such exceptionally favorable trans-actions as these to convince Mathias to make this trip, which was not included in his theoretical itinerary; otherwise two three-hour crossings represented too many complications and too great a loss of time for so small an island—barely two thousand inhabitants—to which nothing else, neither childhood friendships nor early memories of any kind, at-tracted him. The houses on the island were so much alike that he was not even sure he could recognize the one in which he had spent almost his entire childhood and which, unless there was some mistake, was also the house where he had been born.

They assured him that nothing had changed for thirty years, but often a shed added on to a gable or a little stone-work redressed is enough to make a whole building unrecog-nizable. And even supposing that everything, down to the smallest detail, had remained just as he had left it, he would still have to reckon with the errors and inaccuracies of his own memory, which experience had taught him to mistrust. More than any real changes on the island, or even hazy recollections—which were nevertheless numerous enough to prevent him from retaining any precise image of the place —he would have to be wary of exact but false memories which would here and there have substituted themselves for the original earth and stones.

After all, all the houses on the island looked alike: a low door between two small, square windows—and the same arrangement at the back. From one door to the other a tiled hallway split the house down the middle, separating the four rooms into two symmetrical groups: on one side the kitchen and a bedroom, on the other a second bedroom and

a room used either as a parlor or as a kind of lumber room.
The kitchen and bedroom on the street side faced east and
received the morning sun. The remaining two rooms looked
out toward the cliff over three hundred yards of open
ground rolling toward an indentation in the coast. The
winter rains and the west wind battered against the windows; it was only in milder weather that the shutters could
be left open. He had been sitting all afternoon at the heavy
table wedged into the window recess, drawing a sea gull
that had perched on one of the fence posts at the end of the
garden.

Neither the arrangement of the grounds nor their orienta-
tion gave him enough clues. As for the cliff, it was the same
all the way around the island—and the same, moreover, on
the mainland opposite. Its indentations and rises could be
as easily confused as pebbles on a beach, as gray gulls.

Fortunately Mathias did not care much about such matters. He had no intention of looking for the house at the
moor's edge, or for the bird on its perch. He had only made
his inquiries so carefully, the day before, about the forgotten
topography of the island in order to establish the most convenient route, to facilitate broaching the subject of watches
in the houses he was supposed to be returning to with such
understandable pleasure. The extra effort of cordiality—above
all of imagination—required by such an enterprise would
be more than compensated for by the profit of five thousand
crowns he expected to clear.

He really needed the money. For almost three months,
sales had been noticeably below normal; if matters did not
soon improve, he would have to get rid of his stock at cut
prices—probably at a loss—and find another job again. Among
the measures contemplated to settle his difficulties, the imminent canvassing of the island played an important role.
Eighteen thousand crowns in cash at such a time meant

much more than his thirty-per-cent commission: he would not immediately replace all the watches sold, and the sum would permit him to hold out until better days. If this privileged territory had not been originally included in his schedule, it was doubtless because he had wanted to keep it in reserve for bad times. Present circumstances compelled him to make the trip—of which the inconveniences appeared ever more numerous, as he had feared.

The boat left at seven in the morning, which had forced Mathias to get up earlier than usual. When he traveled by bus or the local railroad he almost never started before eight o'clock. Besides, although his house was quite near the train station it was a good distance from the harbor—and none of the bus lines brought him much nearer. He might as well walk the whole way.

At this hour of the morning the Saint-Jacques district was deserted. As he was walking down an alley which he hoped would be a short cut, Mathias thought he heard a moan—faint, yet seeming to come from so near by that he turned his head. There was no one in sight; the street was as empty behind him as in front. He was about to continue on his way when he heard the sound again, a distinct moan almost in his ear. At that moment he noticed a ground-floor window within reach of his right hand; a light was shining inside although by now the daylight was barely obscured by the simple voile curtain that hung behind the panes. The room looked rather large, however, and its only window was of modest size: a yard wide, perhaps, and scarcely any higher; with its four identical, almost square panes it would have been more suitable for a farmhouse than these urban premises. The folds of the curtain made it impossible to see how the room was furnished. All that could be distinguished was what the electric light illuminated at the back of the room: the conical lamp shade—a bed lamp—and the vaguer form of an unmade bed. Standing near the bed, bending slightly over it, a masculine silhouette lifted one arm toward the ceiling.

The whole scene remained motionless. In spite of the incomplete nature of his gesture, the man moved no more than a statue. Under the lamp, on the night table, was a small blue rectangular object—which must have been a pack of cigarettes.

Mathias had no time to wait for what was going to happen next—supposing that anything was going to happen next. He was not even certain the moans came from this house; he had guessed they came from a source still closer, less muffled than they would have been by a closed window. In thinking it over he wondered if he had heard only moans, inarticulate sounds; had there been identifiable words? In any case it was impossible for him to remember what they were. Judging from the quality of her voice—which was pleasant, and not at all sad—the victim must have been a very young woman, or a child. She was standing against one of the iron pillars that supported the deck above; her hands were clasped behind the small of her back, her legs braced and slightly spread, her head leaning against the column. Her huge eyes inordinately wide (whereas all the passengers were squinting because the sun had begun to break through), she continued to look straight ahead of her, with the same calmness with which she had just now looked into his own eyes.

Confronted with such insistence, he had thought at first that the wad of cord belonged to her. She might be making a collection herself. But then he had decided this was an absurd notion: that was no pastime for little girls. Yet boys always have their pockets full of knives, string, chains, and those porous clematis stems they smoke for cigarettes.

Nevertheless, he couldn't recall that his tastes as a collector had been widely encouraged. The good pieces that came into the house were usually confiscated for some domestic purpose. When he complained, they seemed not to understand his disappointment, "since he didn't use them for anything, anyway." The shoebox was in the biggest cupboard of the back room, on a lower shelf; the cupboard was kept locked and he was allowed to have his box only after he had done all his homework and learned his lessons. Sometimes he had to wait several days before he could put a new acquisition in it; meanwhile he carried it in his right pocket, where it kept company with the little brass chain which was a permanent resident there. In these conditions even the best quality cords lost something of their sheen and their cleanness; the most exposed loops blackened, the torsion of the fibers slackened, little threads stuck out everywhere. Continual friction against the metal links must have hastened the fraying process. Sometimes after too long a wait the latest find became good for nothing except tying up packages.

A sudden anxiety crossed his mind: the majority of the pieces kept in the box had been put there without having been in his pocket, or at most after only a few hours of this ordeal. So what confidence could he have in their qualities? Obviously less than in the others. To compensate he would have to subject them to a more rigorous examination. Mathias wanted to take out of his duffle coat the piece of cord rolled into a figure eight in order to estimate its value again. But he couldn't reach his right pocket with his left hand, and his right hand was holding the little suitcase. There was still time to set down the suitcase before becoming involved in the confusion of disembarkation, and even to open it in order to put the cord safely away. The contact with the coins in his pocket would be bad for it. Since Mathias had no need of company to enjoy this pastime of his, he didn't

have to carry the best specimens with him for his school-
mates to admire—he didn't even know whether they would
have liked them at all. Actually, the string other boys filled
their pockets with seemed to have no relation to the string
he collected; in any case, theirs demanded fewer precau-
tions and evidently gave them less trouble. Unfortunately,
the suitcase with the watches in it was not the shoebox; he
tried not to clutter it up with questionable objects that might
produce a bad impression on the clientele when the time
came for him to display his wares. Appearances were more
important than anything else, and he must omit nothing,
leave nothing to chance, if he wanted to sell eighty-nine
wrist watches to slightly less than two thousand people—
including children and paupers.

Mathias tried to divide two thousand by eighty-nine in his
head. He lost his place and decided to use a round number
as his divisor—one hundred, to account for the cottages and
shanties too isolated for him to visit. That would come to
about one sale for every twenty inhabitants—so by supposing
each family to average five people, that would mean one
sale for every four houses visited. Of course he knew from
experience that things turned out differently in practice: in
one family, where they might feel well-disposed toward him,
he sometimes succeeded in selling two or three watches at
a time. Nevertheless, the overall rhythm of one watch for
every four houses would be difficult to attain—difficult, not
impossible.

Today especially, success would be a matter of imagination. He would have to have played, long ago, over there
on the cliff, with many little friends whom he had never
known. Together they would have explored, at low tide,
the unfamiliar regions inhabited by forms of life of only an
equivocal probability. He had taught the others how to
make the sabellas and sea-anemones open. Along the beaches

they had found unidentifiable sea-wrack. For hours at a time they had watched the water rising and falling in the sheltered angle of the landing slip, had watched the seaweed alternately revealed and submerged. He had even showed them his string, had invented all kinds of complicated and uncertain games. People don't remember such things; he would manufacture childhoods for them leading straight to the purchase of a wrist watch. With the young it would be more convenient to have known a mother, a grandfather, or someone else.

A brother and an uncle, for instance. Mathias had reached the pier long before sailing time. He had talked to one of the sailors of the line who like himself, he discovered, had been born on the island; the man's whole family was still living there, his sister in particular, who had three daughters. Two were already engaged, but the third girl was causing her mother many worries. She couldn't be made to behave, and even at her age had an upsetting number of admirers. "She really is a devil," the sailor repeated, with a smile that betrayed how fond he was of his niece in spite of everything. Their house was the last one on the road to the big lighthouse as you left town. His sister was a widow, in easy circumstances. The three girls were named Maria, Jeanne, and Jacqueline. Mathias, who expected to put them to good use soon, added all these facts to the inquiries he had made the day before. In work like his, there was no such thing as a superfluous detail. He decided to have known the brother for a long time; if need be, he would have sold him a "six-jewel" model he had been using for years without it ever needing the slightest adjustment.

When the man made a gesture, Mathias noticed that he was not wearing a watch. His wrists stuck out beyond the sleeves of his jumper when he reached up to fasten the tarpaulin at the back of the post-office van. Nor was there a light strip around the skin of the left wrist, as there would have been if he had been wearing a watch until recently— if it was being repaired, for example. The watch, actually, had never needed repairs. The fact of the matter was that the sailor did not wear it during the week for fear of damaging it while he was working.

The two arms fell back. The man shouted something that was not understood on board over the noise of the engines; at the same moment he stepped to one side of the van and waved to the driver. The van's motor had not stopped, and the vehicle pulled away at once, making a quick, unhesitating turn around the little company office.

The employee in the chevroned helmet who had taken the tickets at the gangplank returned to the company office, closing the door behind him. The sailor who had just cast off the moorings from the pier and tossed them onto the deck took a tobacco pouch out of his pocket and began to roll himself a cigarette. At his right the ship's boy held out his arms, letting them fall slack at a certain distance from his body. The two of them remained alone at the end of the quay, along with the man whose watch worked so perfectly; the latter, noticing Mathias, waved his hand as if to wish him *bon voyage*. The stone rim began its oblique receding movement.

It was exactly seven o'clock. Mathias, whose time had to be very strictly calculated, noticed this with satisfaction. If the fog didn't grow too thick, they would be on time.

In any case, once ashore he mustn't waste a minute; it was the brevity of his stay, made necessary by the rest of his itinerary, which constituted the chief difficulty. It was true that the steamship line was not making his work any easier for him: there were only two boats a week, one making a round trip on Tuesday, the other on Friday. There was no question of staying on the island four days; that would be almost a week, and the whole advantage of his undertaking would be lost, or just about. He would have to confine himself to this one, all-too-short day, between the boat's arrival at ten and its departure at four-fifteen that afternoon. He therefore had six hours and fifteen minutes at his disposal —that would make three hundred sixty plus fifteen, three hundred and seventy-five minutes. Problem: if he wanted to sell his eighty-nine watches, how much time could he allow for each one?

Three hundred seventy-five divided by eighty-nine. . . . By using ninety and three hundred sixty the result was easy: four times nine, thirty-six—four minutes for each watch. Using the actual figures would even give him a little extra time: first of all the fifteen minutes omitted from the calculation, and then the time that the sale of the ninetieth watch (already sold) would have taken—another four minutes—fifteen and four, nineteen—a nineteen-minute margin in order not to risk missing the boat back. Mathias tried to imagine this ideal sale which would last only four minutes: arrival, sales-talk, display of the merchandise, choice of the article, payment of the amount written on the price-tag, departure. Even not taking into account any hesitation on the customer's part, any fuller explanation on his, any discussion about the price, how could he hope to sell everything he had in so little time?

The last house on the road to the big lighthouse as you leave town is an ordinary house: a one-story building with a small, square window on either side of a low door. As he passes Mathias knocks on the pane of the first window and without pausing continues to the door. The second he reaches it, he sees the door open in front of him; there is no need whatever to hesitate before entering the hallway, and then, after a quarter-turn to the right, the kitchen itself, where he immediately sets his suitcase down flat on the big

.th a quick gesture he opens the clasp; the cover
back and right on top can be seen the most expen-
.ems; he seizes the first cardboard strip in his right
. while with his left he lifts the protecting sheet of
,er and points to the three splendid ladies' watches at
.ur hundred twenty-five crowns. The lady of the house is
standing near him, flanked by her two elder daughters (a
little shorter than their mother), all three motionless and
attentive. As one person, with a gesture of rapid, identical,
and perfectly synchronized acquiescence, all three nod their
heads. Already Mathias is removing—almost tearing—from
the cardboard strip the three watches, one after the other,
in order to hold them out to the three women who one after
the other extend their hands—the mother first, then the
daughter on the right, then the daughter on the left.
The amount, calculated in advance, is there on the table:
one thousand-crown note, two hundred-crown notes, and
three twenty-five-crown pieces—twelve hundred seventy-five
crowns—four hundred twenty-five multiplied by three. The
amount is correct. The suitcase closes with a dry click.

As he was leaving he wanted to say a few words of farewell, but none came out of his mouth. He noticed this at
the same moment he realized that the whole scene had been
a stupidly wordless one. Once on the road, behind the closed
door, his suitcase unopened in his hand, he understood that
it all still remained to be done. Turning around, he knocked
with his ring against the door panel, which echoed as if he
had struck an empty box.

The varnished paint, recently renewed, imitated the veins
and irregularities of wood to a fault. Judging from the sound
of his knock, there could be no doubt that under this de-
ceptive layer the door was really a wooden one. On a
level with his face there were two round knots painted side
by side: they looked like two big eyes—or more precisely

like a pair of glasses. They were represented with an attention to detail not generally accorded to this type of decoration; yet although executed with the greatest possible realism, they comprised a perfection of design virtually beyond probability; it must have been artificial because it appeared so studied, as if the accidents themselves had occurred in obedience to law. But it would have been difficult to prove by any particular detail the flagrant impossibility of any such pattern in nature. Even the suspect symmetry of the whole door could be explained by some new development in carpentry. If the paint were scratched away at this very point, two real knots might have been discovered in the wood, knots cut exactly in this shape—or in any case presenting a very similar formation.

The fibers formed two dark circles, thicker at the top and the bottom and provided, at their highest points, with a little excrescence pointing upward. More than like a pair of glasses, they looked like two rings painted in *trompe-l'oeil*, with the shadows they cast on the wood panel and the two nails on which they hung. Their position was certainly surprising, and their modest size seemed out of all proportion to the thickness of the ropes usually used: nothing much heavier than thin cords could have been attached to them.

Because of the green seaweed that grew on the lower section of the landing slip, Mathias was obliged to watch where he put his feet in order not to slip, lose his balance, and do some kind of damage to his precious burden.

After a few steps he was out of danger. Having reached the top of the inclined plane, he continued to make his way along the jetty at the top of the pier extending straight toward the quay. But the crowd of passengers moved very slowly among the nets and traps, and Mathias could not walk as rapidly as he wanted to. To jostle past his neighbors served no purpose, in view of the narrowness and complexity

of the passage. He would have to advance at their pace.
Nevertheless he felt a slight impatience rising within him.
They were taking too long to answer the door. Lifting his
hand on a level with his face this time, he knocked again—
between the two eyes painted on the wood. The door, which
must have been extremely thick, sent back a dull sound
which would be barely audible inside. He was about to
knock again, this time with his ring, when he heard a noise
in the vestibule.

Now he must get something a little less ghostly under
way. It was essential that the customers say something;
therefore he would have to say something first. The exaggerated acceleration of his gestures also constituted a major
danger: working fast must not keep him from remaining
natural.

The door opened on the mother's mistrustful countenance.
Distracted from her work by this unexpected visit and finding herself face to face with a stranger—the island was so
small she knew everyone on it—she was already preparing
to close the door again. Mathias was someone who had
knocked at the wrong door—or else a traveling salesman,
which was no better.

Of course she said nothing. He made what seemed to him
a considerable effort: "Good morning, madame," he said.
"How are you?" The door slammed in his face.

The door had not slammed, but it was still closed. Mathias
felt as if he were going to be dizzy.

He noticed that he was walking too near the edge, on the
side where the pier had no railing. He stopped to let a group
of people pass him; a narrowing of the path, caused by
the accumulation of empty boxes and baskets, dangerously
choked the line of passengers ahead of him. Down the vertical embankment his gaze plunged to the water that rose
and fell against the stone. The pier's shadow colored it a

dark green—almost black. As soon as the path was clear, he stepped away from the edge—to the left—and continued on his way.

A voice behind him repeated that the boat was on time this morning. But this was not quite accurate: it had actually docked a good five minutes late. Mathias turned his wrist to glance at his watch. This whole landing was interminable.

When he finally managed to reach the kitchen, a period of time out of all proportion to the amount at his disposal must have passed, yet he had not promoted his interests in the slightest. The lady of the house had only admitted him, apparently, against her better judgment. He set his suitcase down flat on the big oval table in the middle of the room.

"You can judge for yourself," he forced himself to say; but hearing the sound of his own voice and the silence that followed, he sensed how falsely it rang. The words lacked conviction—density—to a disturbing degree; it was worse than saying nothing at all. The table was covered by an oilcloth with a pattern of little flowers, a pattern that might have been like the one on the lining of his suitcase. As soon as he had opened the suitcase he quickly put the memorandum book inside the open cover, in the hope of concealing the dolls from his customer.

Instead of the memorandum book spread conspicuously over the sheet of paper that protected the first row of watches, appeared the wad of cord rolled into a figure eight. Mathias was in front of the door to the house, contemplating the two circles with their symmetrical deformations painted side by side in the center of the panel. Finally he heard a noise in the vestibule and the door opened on the mother's mistrustful countenance.

"Good morning, madame."

For a moment he thought she was going to answer, but he was mistaken; she continued to look at him without speaking. Her strained, almost anxious expression indicated something more than surprise, something more than ill-humor or suspicion; and if she was frightened, it was difficult to imagine why. Her features were frozen in the very expression they had assumed when she first saw him—as though unexpectedly recorded on a photographic plate. This immobility, far from making it easier to read her countenance, merely rendered each attempt at interpretation more uncertain: although the face, judging from appearances, expressed some intention—a very banal intention that seemed identifiable at first glance—it ceaselessly avoided every reference by which Mathias attempted to capture its meaning. He was not even altogether certain whether she was looking at him —the man who provoked her mistrust, her astonishment, her fear . . . —or at something behind him—beyond the road, the potato field bordering it, the barbed-wire fence, and the open ground on the other side—something that came from the sea.

She didn't appear to see him. He made what seemed to him a considerable effort: "Good morning, madame," he said. "I have news for you . . ."

The pupils of her eyes had not moved a fraction of an inch; yet he had the impression—he imagined the impression, he gathered it, a net full of fish, or of too much seaweed, or of a little mud—he imagined that her gaze fell on him.

The customer was looking at him. "I have some news for you, some news of your brother, your brother the sailor." The woman opened her mouth several times, moving her lips as if she were speaking—with difficulty. But no sound came from them.

Then, very low, a few seconds later, came the words: "I have no brother"—words too brief to correspond to the movements the lips had made a moment before. Immediately afterward—as an echo—came the expected sounds, somewhat more distinct although distorted, inhuman, like the voice of an old phonograph record: "Which brother? All my brothers are sailors."

The eyes had moved no more than the lips. They still looked away, toward the open ground, the cliff, the distant sea beyond the field and the barbed-wire fence.

Mathias, on the verge of abandoning his attempt, started to explain again: he meant the brother who worked for the steamship company. The voice became more regular as it answered: "Oh, of course, that's Joseph." And she asked if there was a message.

From then on, fortunately, the conversation gathered momentum and accelerated. Intonations and expressions began to come into focus; gestures and words were once again functioning almost normally: ". . . wrist watches . . . the finest being manufactured today, and the cheapest as well; all sold with a guarantee and a manufacturer's certificate, registered and trade-marked, waterproof, rustproof, shockproof, antimagnetic . . ." He would have to keep track of the time all this was taking, but at the moment the question of knowing whether the brother wore a watch—and for how long he had—threatened to lead to another collapse. Mathias needed all his attention to get past it.

He managed to reach the kitchen and its oval table, and set his suitcase on it while continuing the conversation. Then there was the oilcloth and the little flowers of its pattern. Things were going almost too quickly. There was the pressure of his fingers on the clasp of the suitcase, the cover opening wide, the memorandum book lying on the pile of cardboard strips, the dolls printed on the lining, the memorandum book inside the open cover, the piece of cord rolled into a figure eight on top of the pile of cardboard strips, the vertical side of the pier extending straight toward the quay. Mathias stepped back from the water, toward the parapet.

Among the passengers lined up in front of him he looked for the little girl who had been staring into space; he did not see her any more—unless he was looking at her without recognizing her. He turned around as he was walking, thinking he might catch sight of her behind him. He was surprised to discover that he was the last passenger on the pier. Behind him the pier was empty again, a cluster of parallel lines describing a series of elongated planes alternately horizontal and vertical, in light and in shadow. At the very end was the beacon light that indicated the entrance to the harbor.

Before reaching the end of the pier, the horizontal plane formed by the jetty underwent a change, lost in an abrupt inset about two-thirds of its width, and continued, thus narrowed, as far as the turret of the beacon light between the massive parapet (on the open sea side) and the embankment without a railing that was set back for two or three yards of its length, plunging straight down into the black water. From where Mathias was standing the landing slip was no longer visible because of the steepness of its slope, so that the jetty appeared to be cut off at that point without any reason.

When he turned around and continued his interrupted walk toward the quay, there was no one on the pier ahead of him either. It was suddenly deserted. On the quay, in front of the row of houses, only three or four little groups of people could be seen, and a few isolated figures moving in one direction or the other, going about their affairs. The men were all wearing more or less worn and patched blue canvas trousers and wide fishermen's jumpers. The women wore aprons and were bare-headed. All had on sabots. These people could not be the passengers who had disembarked to join their families. The passengers had disappeared—had already gone into their houses, or perhaps into the nearby alley leading to the center of town.

But the center of town was not situated behind the houses along the quay. It was a square, opening at its narrowest side on the quay itself and roughly triangular in shape. Besides the quay, which thus constituted the base of the triangle pointing into the town, four roadways opened into it: one into each of the long sides (the least important) of the triangle, and the two others at its point—on the right the road to the fort, which it skirted before following the coast toward the northwest, and on the left the road to the big lighthouse.

In the center of the square Mathias noticed a statue he did not recognize—at least he had no recollection of it. Rising from a granite pedestal cut to imitate living rock, a woman in regional dress (which was no longer worn) was scanning the horizon toward the open sea. Although there was no list of names cut into the sides of the pedestal, the statue must have been a monument to the dead.

As he was passing next to the high iron fence around it —a circle of rectilinear, vertical, and equidistant rails—he saw at his feet, on the big rectangular paving-stones laid around the monument, the shadow of the stone peasant woman. It was deformed in projection, unrecognizable but distinct: very dark in contrast to the rest of the dusty surface and so sharp in outline that Mathias had the sensation of stumbling against a solid body. He made an instinctive movement to avoid the obstacle.

He had not had time yet to begin the necessary swerve when he was already smiling at his mistake. He put his foot in the middle of the body. Around him the fence rails ruled off the ground with the oblique regularity of the heavily lined white paper made for schoolchildren to learn to slant

their handwriting regularly. Mathias turned right to get out
of the network of shadows more quickly. He stepped down
to the uneven cobbles. The sun, as the distinctness of the
shadows bore witness, had burned off the morning mist. At
this season it was unusual that a day promised to be so fine.

The café–tobacco shop, which also served as a garage,
according to the information he had obtained the day before,
was on the right side of the triangle, at the corner of the
alley that led to the quay.

In front of the door a bulletin-board, supported from behind by two wooden uprights, offered the weekly program
of the local movie house. The showings doubtless took place
in the garage itself, on Sundays. In the garishly colored
advertisement, a colossal man dressed in Renaissance clothes
was clutching a young girl wearing a kind of long pale
nightgown; the man was holding her wrists behind her back
with one hand, and was strangling her with the other. The
upper part of her body and her head were bent backward
in her effort to escape her executioner, and her long blond
hair hung down to the ground. The setting in the background represented a tremendous pillared bed with red
covers.

The bulletin-board was placed in such a way—partly concealing the entrance—that Mathias was obliged to walk
around it in order to get into the café. There were no
customers in the room, and no one was behind the counter.
Instead of calling, he came out again after a moment's wait.

No one could be seen in the vicinity. The square itself
gave an impression of solitude. Except for the tobacco shop,
there was not a single store: the grocery, the butcher shop,
the bakery, and the main café all faced the harbor. Furthermore, more than half its left side consisted of an unbroken
wall almost six feet high, its masonry crumbling and its tile
sheathing missing in several places. At the point of the tri-

angle, in the fork of the two roads, stood a small, official-looking building, set off by a plot of ground; above the pediment was a long pole with a flag attached to it; it might have been a school or the town hall—or both. Everywhere (except around the statue), the utter absence of sidewalks was surprising: the roadway of old paving-stones, full of humps and hollows, reached to the house walls. Mathias had forgotten this detail, like everything else. In his round-about inspection, his eyes fell again on the wooden bulletin-board. He had already seen this advertisement a few weeks ago, posted all over the city. Probably its unusual angle made him notice for the first time the broken doll lying on the ground at the hero's feet.

He raised his eyes toward the windows above the café, in the hope of catching someone's attention. The building, al-most austere in its simplicity, had only one upper story, like all its neighbors, whereas most of those facing the harbor had two. He noticed along the alley joining the square the backs of the houses he had already passed in front—their structure was just as elementary, in spite of their greater size. The last, at the corner formed by the square and the quay, stood out in a patch of shadow against the sparkling water of the harbor. The free end of the pier could be seen protruding beyond the gable-end; it too was in shadow, striped with a single horizontal line of light running its length between the parapet and the inner embankment and connected by a short, oblique projection to the ship moored against the landing slip. Farther away than it seemed, and especially by contrast with the pier that was actually larger at low tide, the ship had become ridiculously tiny.

Mathias had to screen his eyes with his hand to protect them from the sun.

Emerging from the angle between the houses, a woman in a black dress with a wide skirt and narrow apron crossed the square in his direction. In order not to have to step up onto the sidewalk around the monument, her path described a curve of which the eventual perfection disappeared in the irregularities of the terrain. When she was no more than two or three steps away Mathias greeted her and asked if she knew where he could find the owner of the garage. He wanted—he added—to rent a bicycle for the day. The woman pointed to the movie advertisement, that is, to the tobacco shop located behind it; then, learning that there was no one inside, she seemed to be distressed by the news, as if in that case the situation was without remedy. To spare his feelings, no doubt, she declared—in very vague terms—that the garageman would not have rented him a bicycle anyway; or else her words must have meant . . .

At this moment a man's head appeared in the doorway above the bulletin-board.

"There," said the woman, "there's someone now." And she disappeared into the alley leading to the harbor. Mathias walked over to the tobacconist.

"Good-looking girl, isn't she?" the man said, with a wink toward the alley.

Although he had seen nothing particularly attractive about the woman in question, who had not seemed to him even very young, Mathias returned the wink—as a professional obligation. In fact it had not even crossed his mind that she might be considered from this point of view; he remembered only that she was wearing a thin black ribbon around her neck, in accordance with the old island custom. He began explaining his business at once. He had been sent by Père Henry, the proprietor of the Café Transatlantique (one of the city's large establishments); he wanted to rent a bicycle for the day—a good bicycle. He would return it at four this afternoon, before the boat left, since he had no intention of staying until Friday.

"Are you a traveling salesman?" asked the man.

"Wrist watches," answered Mathias, lightly tapping his suitcase.

"Ha! Ha! You sell watches," repeated the other. "Good for you!" But immediately afterward, with a grimace: "You won't sell one, they're all too backward around here. You're wasting your time."

"I'll try my luck," answered Mathias good-naturedly.

"All right. Fine. That's up to you. In any case, you wanted a bicycle?"

"Yes, the best one you have."

The garageman thought for a moment and declared that in his opinion there wasn't any need for a bicycle to cover six blocks of houses. He indicated the square with an ironic shrug.

"I'll be working more in the country," explained Mathias. "A kind of specialty."

"Oh, in the country? All right then!" agreed the garageman.

As he spoke these last words he opened his eyes wide: selling watches to the people living on the cliff seemed even more chimerical to him. The conversation nevertheless remained quite friendly—although a little too long for Mathias' taste. His interlocutor had an odd way of answering, always beginning in agreement, even repeating his own words in a tone of conviction, only to introduce some doubt a second later, and then deny everything by a contrary, more or less categorical, proposition.

"Well then," he concluded, "you'll travel around the island. You have good weather for it. Some people think the cliffs are picturesque."

"As for the island, you see, I know it already: I was born here!" replied Mathias.

And as if to prove what he had said, he gave his surname.

This time the garageman started off on still more complicated considerations in which he managed to imply that
Mathias must have been born on the island to conceive the
preposterous notion of returning to it for a sales trip, and
at the same time that the expectation of selling a single
wrist watch betrayed a complete ignorance of the place,
and finally that names like his didn't mean a thing—you
could find them wherever you liked. He himself was not
born on the island—of course not—and he didn't expect to
stay there and "gather moss," either.

As for the bicycle, the man had an excellent one which
wasn't "here, at the moment." He would go fetch it, "as a
favor"; Mathias would have it in half an hour without fail.
Mathias thanked him; he would adapt himself to this turn
of events, would make a quick visit to some of the houses
in town before canvassing the outlying villages, and would
return for the bicycle in exactly three-quarters of an hour.

On the off chance, he offered to display his wares: "excellent merchandise, completely guaranteed and at unbeatable
prices." The other having agreed, they went into the café,
where Mathias opened his suitcase on the first table from
the door. Scarcely had he lifted the paper protecting the
top strip of cardboard than his client changed his mind:
he had no need of a watch, he was wearing one now (he
lifted his sleeve—it was true) and was even keeping another
in reserve. Besides, he would have to hurry if he was to
get hold of the bicycle by the time he had promised. In
his haste he almost pushed the salesman out of the café. It
was as if he had acted as though he had only to verify the
contents of the suitcase. What had he expected to find?

Above the wooden bulletin-board Mathias caught sight
of the granite statue which divided the visible part of the
pier into two sections. He stepped down onto the uneven
cobbles, and in order to avoid the bulletin-board made a

step in the direction of the town hall—of what looked like a town hall—in miniature. If the building had been newer, its size would have made it look like a model.

Then his gaze turned left, sweeping over the whole length of the square: the little plot of ground in front of the town hall, the road to the big lighthouse, the wall with the crumbling sheathing, the alley and the backs of the first houses facing the harbor, the gable-end of the corner house which cast its shadow on the paving-stones, the central section of the pier in shadow above a quadrilateral of sparkling water, the monument to the dead, the little steamer moored against the landing slip defined by a band of light, the free end of the pier with its beacon light, the open sea as far as the horizon.

The cube-shaped pedestal of the monument had no inscription on its southern face either. Mathias had forgotten to buy cigarettes. He would buy them in a moment, on his way back. In the tobacco shop, among all the apéritif advertisements, hung the placard distributed throughout the province by the syndicate of retail jewelers: "Buy your watch at your Jeweler's." There was no jeweler on the island. The tobacconist was prejudiced against the place and its inhabitants. His exclamation about the woman with the black ribbon must have been made ironically—the incomplete beginning of a favorite manner of speaking:

"Good-looking girl, isn't she?"

"That one, yes! Good enough to eat!"

"Well, you're not hard to please! They're all hideous around here, and drunk all the time."

The fellow's pessimistic predictions ("You won't sell one, they're all too backward around here!") were nevertheless a bad omen. Without conceding them any objective importance—without believing they corresponded to any real knowledge, on the part of the speaker, of the market, or even to any particular power of divination—Mathias would have preferred not having heard them. Then too, he still felt a certain annoyance at the recent decision to begin his rounds in town, when according to the original itinerary he would have completed his rounds there—if the country left him time enough before the boat's departure. His confidence—carefully constructed but entirely too fragile—was already shaken. He tried to find in this vacillation—in this propitiatory change of plan—some token of success, but in reality he felt the whole enterprise collapsing beneath him.

He was going to start out now by devoting three-quarters of an hour to these sad houses, where he was positive he would meet with one failure after another. When he would finally leave on the bicycle, it would be after eleven. From eleven to four-fifteen left only five and a quarter hours— three hundred fifteen minutes. Furthermore, it wasn't four minutes per sale that he would have to allow, but ten at least. By putting every one of his three hundred fifteen minutes to good advantage he would still only manage to get rid of thirty-one and a half watches. And unfortunately even this result was inaccurate: first of all he would have to subtract the considerable amount of time spent in getting from place to place and then, above all, the time wasted on people who didn't buy anything—obviously the most numerous. According to his most favorable calculations (those by which he sold all eighty-nine watches), out of the two thousand inhabitants there were in any case nineteen hundred eleven who would refuse to buy; figuring even only a minute per person, that came to nineteen hundred eleven minutes, which—dividing by sixty—was more than thirty hours for refusals alone. It was five times more time than he had! One-fifth of a minute—twelve seconds —twelve seconds for a negative answer. He might as well give up right away, since he didn't even have time to free himself from so many refusals.

Along the quay in front of him stretched the housefronts which led him back toward the pier. The vague light brought no detail into relief, nothing solid to hold on to. The crumbling whitewashed walls, stained with damp, were of no age and of no period. The clump of buildings did not suggest much of the island's former importance—an entirely military importance, it was true, but one which in past centuries had permitted the development of a flourishing little port. After the naval services' abandonment of a base impossible to defend against modern weapons, a fire had completed the ruin of the decaying town. The dwellings built in place of those destroyed were much less luxurious and no longer on the same scale as the immense pier, which now protected no more than twenty small sailboats and a few trawlers of low tonnage, and bore no relation to the imposing mass of the fort which marked the town limit on the other side. It was now nothing more than an extremely modest fishing port, with neither natural resources nor commercial possibilities. Shellfish and the fish taken by trawler were shipped to the mainland, but the profits from this trade grew less and less satisfactory. The spider-crabs that were a specialty of the island sold particularly badly.

At low tide the remains of these crabs strewed the naked mud in front of the quay. Among the flat stones with their manes of rotting seaweed, on the barely slanting blackish surface, in which sparkled here and there a tin can that still had not rusted, a bit of crockery painted with little flowers, a blue enamel skimmer almost intact, their arched, spiny shells could be distinguished next to the longer, smoother shells of ordinary crabs. There was also a considerable quantity of bony legs, or parts of legs—one, two, or three joints ending in a claw that was too long, slightly curved, and sharp-edged—and large, pointed pincers, most of them broken, some of startling size, worthy of real sea monsters. Under the morning sun the whole surface gave off an odor that was already strong, though not quite repellent: a mixture of iodine, fuel oil, and slightly stale shrimp.

Mathias, who had stepped out of his path to get nearer the edge, turned back toward the houses. He crossed the width of the quay toward the shop forming the corner of the square—a kind of dry goods-hardware emporium—and entered the dark orifice that opened between it and the butcher shop.

The door, which he had found ajar, closed softly as soon as he released it. Coming in out of the bright sunshine, he could see nothing at all for a moment. Then he realized he was looking at the hardware shopwindow from behind. He noticed on the left a round, long-handled enameled iron skimmer like the one sticking out of the mud, the same shade of blue, scarcely any newer. Looking more closely, he discovered that a sizable chip of the enamel had flaked off, leaving a fan-shaped black mark fringed with concentric lines that faded out toward the edge. To the right, a dozen identical little knives—mounted on a cardboard strip, like watches—formed a circle, all pointing toward a tiny design in the center which must have been the manufacturer's trade-mark. Their blades were about four inches long, quite thick but tapering to a sharp cutting edge much slenderer than those of ordinary knives; they were more like triangular stilettos, with a single honed edge. Mathias could not remember ever having seen knives like them; the fishermen doubtless used them for a particular kind of dismemberment—a very ordinary kind, though, since there was no indication as to their use. The cardboard strip was decorated with a red frame, the trade-mark "Indispensable" inscribed at the top in capital letters, and the label at the center of the wheel of which the knives constituted the spokes. The design represented a tree with a smooth, recti-linear trunk terminating in two branches forming a Y and bearing little tufts of foliage that barely protruded beyond the two branches at the sides, but filled in the fork of the Y.

Again Mathias found himself out in the road that had no sidewalk. Of course he had not sold a single wrist watch. In the hardware shopwindow could be seen various objects that were ordinarily sold in dry-goods stores as well, rang-ing from big balls of thread for mending fishnets to black silk braids and pincushions.

Once past the butcher shop, Mathias disappeared into the next doorway.

He made his way down the same dark narrow corridor the arrangement of which he now recognized. Without, however, achieving any greater success. At the first door he knocked on, there was no answer. At the second, a very old woman, pleasant enough although stone deaf, obliged him to abandon all attempts at salesmanship: since she understood nothing of what he wanted, he retreated with many smiles and an expression indicating he was entirely satisfied with his visit; somewhat startled, the old woman decided to smile back and even to thank him warmly. With many reciprocal little bows, they parted after an affectionate handshake; in another moment she would have kissed him. He climbed the uncomfortable staircase to the first floor; there a woman shut the door in his face without giving him time to speak a word; a baby was screaming somewhere. On the second floor he found only some dirty, frightened children—perhaps they were sick, since they were home from school on a Tuesday.

On the quay again, he turned back to try to interest the

butcher, who was waiting on two customers; no one paid enough attention to what he was saying to justify even opening the suitcase. He did not insist, repelled by the cold smell of the meat.

The next shop was the café "A l'Espérance." He walked in. The first thing to do in a café is to buy a drink. He went to the bar, set his suitcase on the floor between his feet, and asked for an absinthe.

The girl working behind the bar had a timorous face and the ill-assured manner of a dog that had been whipped. When she ventured to raise her eyelids her large eyes could be seen—dark and lovely—but only for an instant; she lowered them immediately, leaving only her long doll's lashes to be admired. Their delicate outlines emphasized her vulnerable expression.

Three men—three sailors—whom Mathias had passed as they were arguing in front of the door walked in and sat down at a table. They ordered red wine. The barmaid walked around the bar, awkwardly carrying the bottle and three glasses stacked one inside the other. Without a word she set down the glasses in front of the customers. To fill them exactly she leaned forward from the waist, her head to one side. Under her apron she was wearing a black dress cut low over the delicate skin of her back. Her hair was arranged so that the nape of her neck was completely exposed.

One of the sailors had turned toward the bar. Mathias, without having had time to realize what made him turn away, suddenly wheeled back to his glass of absinthe and drank a swallow of it. In front of him was someone new, standing against the door frame of the inner room, near the cash drawer. Mathias made a vague gesture of greeting.

The man did not seem to notice it. He kept his eyes fastened on the girl who was still pouring the wine.

She was not used to the job. She poured too slowly, constantly watching the level of the liquid in the glass, determined not to waste a drop. When the third one was filled to the brim she raised the bottle and, holding it in both hands, returned to her place with lowered eyes. At the other end of the bar the man watched her severely as she approached him, walking with short steps. She must have become aware of her master's presence—in a flicker of her lashes—for she stopped short, hypnotized by the floorboards at the tips of her shoes.

The others were already quite motionless. Once the girl's change of position—too uncertain to last under such conditions—had been reabsorbed in its turn, the entire scene crystallized.

No one said anything.

The barmaid looked at the floor in front of her feet. The proprietor looked at the barmaid. Mathias watched the proprietor looking at her. The three sailors looked at their glasses. Nothing revealed the pulsation of the blood through the veins—not a quiver.

It would be pointless to try to estimate the time this lasted.

Four syllables rang out. But instead of breaking the silence, they were completely assimilated by it: "Are you asleep?"

The voice was heavy, deep, slightly singsong. Although spoken without anger, almost softly, the words concealed beneath their pretended gentleness an unspecified threat. Or it might have been in this very appearance of intimidation, on the other hand, that the pretense was to be found.

After a considerable delay—as if the command had taken a long time to reach her across a stretch of sand and stagnant water—the girl continued to advance timorously without lifting her head toward the man who had just spoken. (Had anyone seen his lips move?) Having reached a point near him—less than a step away—within reach of his hand—she leaned over to put the bottle back in place—presenting the nape of her neck from which, where it was exposed by her dress, protruded the tip of a vertebra. Then, straightening up, she busied herself drying the newly-washed glasses. Outside, behind the glass door, beyond the paving-stones and the mud, the water of the harbor sparkled in dancing flashes: undulating lozenges of flame forming transverse gothic arches, lines which suddenly contracted to produce a jagged flash of light—which as suddenly flattened, extending horizontally until it formed a line that broke once more into a brilliant zigzag—a jig-saw puzzle, a seamless series of incessant dislocations.

At the sailors' table, air whistled between clenched teeth —preceding the imminent return of speech.

Passionately, though in an undertone, syllables picked out by one: ". . . would deserve . . ." began the youngest, who was continuing some long-drawn-out argument begun elsewhere. "She deserves . . ." A silence. . . . A little whistle. . . . Squinting from the effort of choosing his words, he was looking into a dark corner where the pin-ball machine stood. "I don't know what she deserves."

"Oh, yes!" said one of the two others—the one next to him—in a more sonorous tone, exaggeratedly drawling the initial interjection.

The third sailor, sitting opposite, drank off the wine left in the bottom of his glass and said calmly, already bored by the subject: "A good smack. . . . And you too."

They stopped talking. The proprietor had disappeared from the doorway to the inner room. Mathias noticed the girl's large dark eyes—in a flicker of her lashes. He drank a swallow of absinthe. The glasses were all dried now; to give herself something to do the girl put her hands behind her back on the pretext of retying her apron strings.

"The whip!" continued the young man's voice. He whistled between his teeth, two short blasts, and repeated the word in a more uncertain tone—as if in a dream.

Mathias looked down at the glass of cloudy yellow alcohol in front of him. He saw his right hand lying on the edge of the counter, the nails he had neglected to cut, and their abnormal length and pointedness.

He thrust his hand into the pocket of his duffle coat, where it came in contact with the wad of cord. He remembered the suitcase at his feet, the purpose of his trip, the urgency of his work. But the proprietor was not there any longer and the girl would not be in a position to spend one hundred fifty or two hundred crowns. Two of the drinkers evidently belonged to the non-watch-buying category; as for the youngest, he was repeating some story of an unfaithful wife or fickle sweetheart from which it would be difficult to distract him.

Mathias finished his absinthe and signaled that he was ready to pay for it by jingling the coins in his pocket.

"That will be three crowns seven," said the girl.

Surprisingly enough, she spoke quite naturally, without a trace of embarrassment. The absinthe was not expensive. He spread out on the counter the three silver coins and the seven bronze ones, then added a brand-new half-crown.

"For you."

"Thank you, sir." She picked up all the coins and dropped them pell-mell into the cash drawer.

"Your mistress isn't here?" asked Mathias.

"She's upstairs, sir," the girl answered.

The proprietor's silhouette appeared again in the doorway to the inner room, exactly where it had been before—not in the center, but leaning against the right side—as if he had not moved since his first appearance. His expression had

not changed either: inscrutable, harsh, waxen, it could be
variously interpreted as hostility, concern, or merely absent-
mindedness; on the other hand, such a countenance was
just as likely to harbor the most sinister intentions. The girl
had bent down to stack the clean glasses under the counter.
On the other side of the glass door reflections from the water
flickered in the sunlight.

"Nice day!" said Mathias.

He stooped and picked up his suitcase with his left hand.
He was anxious to get outside again. If no one answered
him he would leave without making further efforts.

Just then came the girl's quiet voice: "This gentleman
wanted to see Madame Robin." In the sun's glare the water
of the harbor danced with dazzling flashes of light. Mathias
put his right hand over his eyes.

"What about?" asked the proprietor.

Mathias turned to face him. He was a tall, heavily built
man—almost a giant. The impression of strength he produced was emphasized by an immobility that he seemed
to find difficult to overcome.

"This is Monsieur Robin," the girl explained.

Mathias nodded his head with a good-natured smile. This
time the proprietor returned his greeting, though with an
almost imperceptible gesture. He must have been about
Mathias' age.

"I once knew someone named Robin," Mathias said, "about
thirty years ago, when I was still just a boy . . ." And he
began to conjure up, in a rather vague way, schoolday
memories suitable to any islander's childhood. "Robin," he
added, "a big, strong fellow. . . . I think he was named
Jean—Jean Robin . . ."

"My cousin," the man said, nodding his head. "He wasn't
so big as all that. Anyway, he's dead."

"No!"

"He died in thirty-six."

"That's incredible!" Mathias exclaimed, suddenly over-come with sadness. His friendship for this imaginary Robin was sensibly enhanced by the fact that he ran no risk of encountering him in the course of his inventions. He men-tioned his own surname in passing and attempted to draw out his interlocutor, who would then take him into his confidence. "And how did the poor chap die?"

"Is that why you wanted to see my wife?" inquired the genuine Robin, whose perplexity might have been authentic.

Mathias reassured him. The purpose of his visit was quite different: he was selling wrist watches and he happened to have with him three attractive ladies' styles which would certainly interest a woman of taste like Madame Robin.

Monsieur Robin made a little gesture with his arm—his first actual movement since his appearance—to show he was not taken in by the compliment. The salesman gave a know-ing laugh which unfortunately aroused no response. At the sailors' table the red-faced man sitting at the deceived lover's left repeated his drawled "oh, yes"—for no apparent reason, since no one had spoken to him. Mathias hastened to explain that he also had a number of men's models of exceptional quality, considering their price—defying all com-petition. He should have opened his suitcase unhesitatingly and enumerated the advantages of his merchandise while passing it around; but the counter was too high to facilitate such an operation, which required freedom of movement, and the use of one of the tables would oblige him to turn his back to the proprietor, his only likely customer. Never-theless, he decided on this unsatisfactory solution and began his sales-talk—standing too far to one side, however, to be in a position to convince any of his hearers. After having washed, dried, and put away his empty glass, the barmaid took a rag and wiped off the counter's zinc top at the spot where he had just been drinking. Next to him the three sailors had begun a new argument as incoherent as the last, with the same economy of words and the same deliberation, displaying neither progression nor conclusion. This time it was something about a shipment of spider-crabs ("hookers," they called them) to be transported to the mainland; there was a disagreement about how they were to be marketed—a difference of opinion, it appeared, with their fishmonger. Or else they were in agreement but not altogether satisfied with the decision they had reached. To put an end to the discussion, the oldest—who was facing the other two—declared that it was his round next. The girl again picked up the bottle of red wine and walked around the bar, taking short steps.

Mathias, who had approached the proprietor in order to give him a better look at one of the series of watches (at two hundred fifty crowns), saw the man's eyes shift from the cardboard strip to the table where his employee was pouring the wine. She held her head to one side, neck and shoulders bent, in order to observe more closely the rising level of the liquid in the glass. Her black dress was cut low in back. Her hair was arranged so that the nape of her neck was exposed.

Since no one was paying attention to him any more, Mathias was about to put the cardboard strip back in the suitcase. The red-faced sailor looked up and made a sudden grimace of complicity in his direction. At the same time he nudged the man next to him: "What about you, Louis, don't you want a watch? Don't you? (A wink.) What about a present for Jacqueline?"

As if in answer the young man whistled between his teeth, two short blasts. The girl suddenly straightened up, twisting at the waist. For an instant Mathias saw her pupils and the dark reflections in the iris of her eyes. She turned on her heels like a marionette, then took the bottle back behind the bar, resuming her slow, delicate doll's gait which he had at first attributed to clumsiness—mistakenly, in all probability.

Mathias also turned around, offering the proprietor a series of ladies' watches: the "*fantasies.*"

"And here's something for Madame Robin; I'm sure she'd like one of these! The first one here is two hundred seventy-five crowns. This one, with the antique case, is three hundred forty-nine. A watch like this is worth at least five hundred crowns at any jeweler's you can name. And I'll include the band as a special gift bonus! Now this one is a real gem!"

His enthusiasm went for nothing. Hardly aroused, his assumed good humor faded of its own accord. The atmosphere was too unfavorable. There was no use persisting under these conditions. No one was listening to him.

Yet on the other hand, no one had explicitly refused him. Perhaps they counted on letting him continue until nightfall, glancing inattentively at his watches and answering with a word or two now and then to keep him from leaving. It would be better to go right away: after all, a ceremony of refusal was not indispensable.

"If you want to," the proprietor said at last, "you can go upstairs. She won't buy anything, but it will give her something to do."

Thinking the husband would accompany him, Mathias was already casting about for an excuse to leave when he realized that the man had no such intention: the proprietor was, in fact, giving him directions for finding his wife, who was occupied, he said, either in the kitchen or with the housework, which made the notion that she needed something to do a rather strange one. In any case, Mathias decided to make a final attempt, hoping to revive his means of persuasion once out of this impassive giant's hearing. Until now he had had the constant sense of talking in a void—a hostile void that devoured his words as soon as he had uttered them.

He closed his suitcase and headed toward the back of the room. Instead of leaving by the door behind the bar, he had been directed to another exit, a doorway in the corner where the pin-ball machine stood.

When the door closed behind him, he was standing in a rather dirty vestibule dimly lighted by a little glass door opening on an interior court, itself deep and dark. The walls around him, once painted a uniform yellow-ochre, were filthy, scaling, scored, even split in places. The wood of the floors and stairs, although evidently as worn by frequent washing as by the passage of feet, was black with encrusted grime. Various objects were piled in the corners: cases of empty bottles, large boxes of corrugated cardboard, a washing-machine, fragments of cast-off furniture. It was apparent they had been stored with a certain system, and had not accumulated merely in successive rejections. Furthermore, nothing was actually dirty; everything seemed quite ordinary: it was obvious that the floorboards simply had not been waxed (which, after all, was not surprising) and that the walls needed repainting. As for the dead silence, that was much less depressing—and more justified —than the virtually mute tension that filled the café from one moment to the next.

A narrow hallway turned off to the right, doubtless leading to the room behind the bar and, farther on, to the quay itself. There were also two stairways, one as narrow as the other—it was difficult to account for both, since they did not appear to lead to different wings of the building.

Mathias was to take the one directly in front of him as he came out of the café; to a certain degree either stairway might have fit this description, although neither of them satisfied it altogether. He hesitated a few seconds and ended by choosing the one farthest from him because the other was distinctly recessed in the wall. He walked up one flight. Here he was confronted by two doors—as he had been told—one with no knob.

The second was not closed, but merely resting against the jamb. He knocked without pressing too heavily, lest the door open completely, for he could feel that it would turn on its hinges at the slightest pressure.

He waited. There was not enough light on the landing for him to tell whether the door was painted to imitate the texture of wood, or else spectacles, eyes, rings, or a whorl of thread rolled into a figure eight.

He knocked again, this time with his ring. As he feared, the door opened by itself. Then he realized that it led only to another vestibule. After waiting again he stepped forward, no longer certain where to knock. There were now three doors in front of him.

The one in the middle was wide open. What it presented to view was not the kitchen described by the proprietor, but a spacious bedroom that surprised Mathias by its resemblance to something he could not later identify. The entire center of the room had been cleared so that the black and white tile flooring was immediately noticeable: white octagons the size of plates, adjacent on four of their sides and thus providing for an equal number of smaller black squares between them. Mathias then recalled that it was an old island custom to lay tiles rather than floorboards in the finest rooms of the house—but more often in the dining room or the living room than in a bedroom. Yet this room left no doubt about its function: a large, low bed filled one of its corners, its long side against the wall facing the door. Against the wall at the right, perpendicular to the head of the bed, a night table supported a bed lamp.

Next came a closed door, then the dressing table over which
hung an oval mirror. A bedside rug made of lambskin
completed the furnishings of this corner. To see farther
along the wall at the right he would have had to put his
head all the way into the room. Similarly, the whole left
side of the room remained concealed by the door to the
vestibule where Mathias was standing.

The tiles on the floor were perfectly clean. No mark soiled
the white, dull, even, apparently new tiles. The whole
room had a neat, almost coquettish look (despite a certain
strangeness) in contrast to the appearance of the stairs and
the hallway.

The tiling alone could not account for the rather unusual
character of the room; its colors were quite ordinary and
its presence in a bedroom was easily explained: for instance,
as a result of a modification of the entire apartment which
had caused the functions of certain rooms to be exchanged.
The bed, the night table, the little rectangular rug, the
dressing table with its mirror were all popular styles, as
was the wallpaper of tiny, many-colored bouquets printed
on a cream-colored background. Over the bed, an oil painting (or a vulgar reproduction framed as if it were a master-
piece) showed the corner of a room just like the one in
which it hung: a low bed, a night table, a lambskin. Kneeling
on the lambskin and facing the bed, a little girl in a nightgown is about to say her prayers, bending her head over
her clasped hands. It is evening. The lamp illuminates,
from a forty-five-degree angle, the child's neck and right
shoulder.

On the night table, the bed lamp had been turned on
—forgotten; the daylight, barely obscured by a simple voile
curtain, had prevented Mathias from noticing it right away,
but the conical lamp shade was unmistakably illuminated

from within. Just beneath it shone a small blue rectangular object—which must have been a pack of cigarettes.

Although the rest of the room seemed orderly enough, the bed looked as if it had been the scene of a struggle, or were in the process of being changed. The dark red bedspread had been rumpled and trailed along the tiles on one side of the bed.

A mild warmth emanated from the room, as if something were still burning in the fireplace, even at this time of year —something not visible from the open door of the vestibule where Mathias was standing.

Toward the other end of the landing was an empty garbage pail and, farther on, two brooms leaning against the wall. At the foot of the stairs he decided not to take the narrow hallway which—he assumed—would lead directly back to the quay. He returned to the café which was now quite empty. He quickly reassured himself: no one would have bought anything, neither the sailors, nor the proprietor, nor the girl with the timorous expression who was probably not in the least timorous, nor awkward, nor even obedient. He opened the glass door and was once again out on the uneven cobbles in front of the sparkling water of the harbor.

The weather was even warmer now. His wool-lined duffle coat began to feel heavy. It was really a lovely day for April.

But he had already wasted too much time and did not loiter warming himself in the sunshine. Turning his back on the edge of the quay overhanging the exposed strip of mud strewn with crabs and dismembered pincers, toward which he had just taken a few steps while thinking of something else, Mathias returned to the row of housefronts and to the uncertain exercise of his profession.

A reddish shop-front. . . . A glass door. . . . He turned the handle mechanically and found himself in the next shop, which had a low ceiling and was darker than its neighbors. A customer, leaning on the counter opposite the saleswoman, was checking a long bill which the saleswoman was adding up on a very small rectangle of white paper. He said nothing lest they lose their place in the calculation. The shopkeeper, who was murmuring her figures in an undertone while following them with the point of her pencil, interrupted herself for a moment to smile at the new customer and to ask him, with a gesture of her hand, to be patient. She immediately plunged back into her calculations. She went so rapidly that Mathias wondered how the customer managed to check her figures. Besides, she must have been quite inaccurate, for she started the same series of numbers several times, and could not seem to reach the end of it. Having said "forty-seven" more loudly, she wrote something on the paper.

"Five!" protested the customer.

They checked the suspect column of figures once again, in chorus now and aloud, but at a still more dizzying speed: "Two and one three and three six and four ten. . . ." The shop was filled with various items of merchandise stacked in bins and racks from floor to ceiling along all four walls; shelves had also been installed behind the modest panes forming the shopwindow—which added considerably to the room's darkness. Baskets and cases were heaped all over the floor; the two long counters, arranged in an *L* filling the rest of the space, were invisible beneath piles of various objects—with the single exception of a two-foot-square surface on which gleamed the rectangle of white paper the two women were leaning over from opposite sides.

The most unrelated articles were piled side by side in great confusion. There were gumdrops, chocolate bars, jars of jam; there were wooden toys and canned goods; a basketful of eggs had been left on the floor; next to it, on a wicker tray, gleamed a spindle-shaped fish, stiff, blue, as long as a dagger, and striped with wavy lines. But there were also pens, books, shoes, espadrilles, even bolts of cloth. And there were still other things of so disparate a nature that Mathias wondered what was written on the shop's signboard outside. In one corner, at eye level, stood a window mannequin: a young woman's body with the limbs cut off —the arms just below the shoulder and the legs eight inches from the trunk—the head slightly to one side and forward to give a "gracious" effect, and one hip projecting slightly beyond the other in a "natural" pose. The mannequin was well-proportioned but smaller than normal, as far as the mutilations permitted her size to be estimated. Her back was turned, her face leaning against a shelf filled with ribbons. She was dressed only in a brassiere and a narrow garter-belt popular in the city.

"Forty-five!" cried out the saleswoman in a triumphant tone. "You're right." And she attacked the next column of figures.

Above the thin silk strap across the back, the smooth golden skin of the shoulders glistened softly. The tip of a vertebra formed a slight eminence at the fragile nape of the neck.

"There you are!" cried out the saleswoman. "We got there all the same."

Mathias' eyes swept over a number of bottles, then a row of jars of several colors, and came to rest on the shopkeeper after having described a half-circle. The customer had straightened up and was looking at him intently from behind her spectacles. Taken unawares, he could not remember what to say in such a situation.

He could manage only gestures: he set down the suitcase on the free surface of the counter and opened the clasp. He quickly took out the black memorandum book to put inside the open cover. He still had not spoken a word when he lifted the paper protecting the first series of watches—the "luxury" models.

"One moment, please," said the shopkeeper with an engaging smile. Turning to the shelves she leaned over, cleared the floor in front of the drawers that lined the lower section of the wall, opened one of them, and with a triumphant expression produced a cardboard strip of ten wrist watches absolutely identical to the ones he had just revealed. This time the situation was certainly unforeseen: with all the more reason Mathias still found nothing to say. He put his merchandise back in the suitcase and placed the memorandum book on top. Before closing the cover he had time to glance at the bright-colored dolls printed on the lining.

"Give me a quarter-pound of gumdrops," he said.

"Certainly. Which ones would you like?" She recited a list of flavors and prices, but without paying any attention to her words he indicated the jar containing the most brightly-colored paper wrappers.

She weighed out four ounces and handed him the little cellophane bag which he put in the right pocket of his duffle coat, where the gumdrops joined the slender hemp cord. He paid and went out.

He was staying too long in the shops. It was easy enough to go in—they opened directly off the road, like country houses—and yet in each one he had to wait several minutes because of the customers, only to be disappointed in the end.

Fortunately a series of private houses succeeded this last shop. Deciding not to explore the latter's first floor which he supposed to be the gumdrop-seller's apartment, he passed down the row.

Along dark hallways lined with closed doors, up narrow stairways leading to failure after failure, he lost himself again among his specters. At one end of a filthy landing he knocked with his ring at a door with no knob which opened by itself. . . . The door swung open and a mistrustful face appeared in the opening—which was just wide enough for him to recognize the black and white tiles on the floor. . . . The large squares were of a uniform gray; the room he entered was not at all remarkable—except for an unmade bed with a red spread trailing on the floor. . . . There was no red bedspread, nor was there an unmade bed; no lambskin, no night table, no bed lamp; there was no blue pack of cigarettes, no flowered wallpaper, no painting on the wall. The room he had been directed to was only a kitchen where he put his suitcase flat on the big oval table in the middle. Then came the oilcloth, the pattern on the oilcloth, the click of the copper-plated clasp, etc. . . .

Emerging from a last shop, one so dark he had been able to see nothing at all—and perhaps hear nothing as well—he realized that he had reached the end of the quay at the point where the long pier began, leading almost perpendicularly from the quay in a cluster of parallel lines to the beacon light where they appeared to converge: two horizontal planes in sunlight alternating with two vertical planes in shadow.

This was where the town ended as well. Mathias had not sold a single watch, and it would be the same story in the three or four alleys behind the quay. He forced himself to take comfort in the fact that his specialty was really the country; the town, no matter how small, doubtless required other qualities than those he possessed. The jetty on top of the pier was deserted. He was about to walk down it when he noticed in front of him an opening in the massive parapet extending right from the end of the quay to an old, half-demolished wall, apparently the remains of the ancient royal city.

Beyond this wall, with little or no transition, stretched a

low, rocky coast—large, gently inclined banks of gray stone sloping into the water without showing any sand, even at low tide.

Mathias walked down the several granite steps that led to the flat rocks. On his left he now noticed the exterior side of the pier—vertical, but in sunlight—a single plane, the parapet joining its base without a discernible seam. As long as his progress was more or less unimpeded he continued to advance toward the sea; but he soon had to stop, not daring to jump over a fault in the rock, though not a large one, encumbered as he was with his heavy shoes, his duffle coat, and his precious suitcase.

He therefore sat down on the rock, facing into the sun, and set down his suitcase near him, wedged between the stones to prevent it from slipping. In spite of the breeze that blew more strongly here, he unbuckled his duffle coat and spread it wide on either side. Mechanically he felt for his wallet in the inside left pocket of his jacket. The sun, dazzlingly reflected from the surface of the water, forced him to keep his eyes more than half-closed. He recalled the little girl on the deck of the ship who kept her eyes wide open and her head raised—her hands behind her back. She looked as if she were bound to the iron pillar. He thrust his hand again into the inside pocket of his jacket and took out the wallet to see if it still contained the newspaper article clipped the day before from the "Western Lighthouse," one of the local dailies. After all, there was no reason why the clipping should not be there. Mathias put the wallet back where it had been.

A little wave broke against the rocks at the foot of the slope and moistened the stone at a level where it had previously been quite dry. The tide was coming in. One gull, two gulls, then a third, passed one after another, coasting slowly on the wind—motionless. Again he saw the iron

rings in the embankment, alternately revealed and submerged by the water that rose and fell in the sheltered angle
of the landing slip. The last bird, suddenly interrupting its
horizontal trajectory, fell like a stone, broke the surface of
the water, and disappeared. A little wave broke against the
rock with a slapping sound. Again he was standing in the
narrow vestibule before the door that opened into the room
with the black and white tiles.

The girl with the timorous expression was sitting on the
edge of the unmade bed, her bare feet resting on the lambskin. On the night table the little lamp was turned on.
Mathias thrust his hand into the inside pocket of his jacket
and took out the wallet. He removed the newspaper clipping, put the wallet back, and once again read the text
attentively from beginning to end.

The article did not have much of importance to say. It
was no longer than a minor news item. In fact a good half
of it merely traced the secondary circumstances of the
discovery of the body; since the entire conclusion of the
article was devoted to commentaries on the direction the
police expected their investigations to take, very little space
remained for the description of the body itself and none at
all for any discussion of the kind of violence to which the
victim had been subjected. Adjectives such as "horrible,"
"unspeakable," and "odious" were of no use in these matters.
Vague laments over the girl's tragic fate were scarcely more
helpful. As for the veiled formulas used to describe the
manner of her death, all belonged to the conventional lan-
guage of the press for this category of news and referred, at
best, to generalities. It was evident that the copy writers
used the same terms on each similar occasion, without
attempting to furnish the slightest piece of real information
in a particular case, concerning which they were probably
in complete ignorance themselves. The scene would have

to be re-invented from beginning to end, starting with two or three elementary details, like the age of the victim or the color of her hair.

A little wave broke against the rock at the foot of the slope, a few yards away from Mathias. His eyes were beginning to hurt. He turned away from the water and walked up the rocks to where a narrow customs road followed the coast southward. The sunlight here had the same blinding intensity. He closed his eyes tight. On the other side, behind the parapet, the flat housefronts extended along the quay as far as the triangular square and its monument encircled with an iron fence. On this side was the succession of shopwindows: the hardware store, the butcher shop, the café "A l'Espérance." That was where he had drunk his absinthe, at the bar, for three crowns seven.

He is on the first floor, standing in the narrow vestibule before the door opening into the room with the black and white tiles. The girl is sitting on the edge of the unmade bed, her bare feet deep in the fleece of the lambskin. Near her the red bedspread is trailing along the floor.

It is night. Only the little lamp on the night table is turned on. For a long moment the scene remains motionless and silent. Then once again the words: "Are you asleep?" are spoken by the heavy, deep, slightly singsong voice which seems to conceal an unspecified threat. Mathias then notices, framed in the oval mirror above the dressing table, the man standing on the left side of the room. His eyes are fixed on something, but the presence of the mirror between him and the observer prevents any accurate surmise as to the direction of his gaze. Her eyes still lowered, the girl stands up and begins to walk timorously toward the man who has just spoken. She leaves the visible part of the room to appear, several seconds later, in the oval mirror. Having reached a

point near her master—less than a step away—within reach
of his hand—she stops.

The giant's hand approaches slowly and comes to rest on
the fragile nape of her neck. It shapes itself around the neck
and presses down, without apparent effort but with so per-
suasive a force that it obliges the entire delicate body to
give way little by little. Bending her knees, the girl puts
down first one foot, then the other, until she is kneeling on
the tiled floor—white octagons the size of plates, adjacent on
four of their sides and thus providing for an equal number
of smaller black squares between them.

The man, who has loosened his hold, is still murmuring
five or six syllables in the same low voice—but muffled,
almost hoarse this time: unintelligible. After a considerable
delay—as if the command had taken a long time to reach
her across a stretch of sand and stagnant water—she gently
begins to move her arms; her small, compliant hands rise
along her thighs, pass behind her hips and finally stop at
the small of her back a little below her waist—her wrists
crossed as if bound. Then the voice can be heard saying
"You are beautiful . . ." with a kind of restrained violence;
and again the giant's fingers fall upon his prey who now
lies at his feet—so small as to seem almost deformed.

His fingertips trail over the naked skin of her neck, along
the nape that is completely exposed by the arrangement of
the hair; then his hand slides under her ear to stroke her
mouth and face in the same way, finally forcing her to lift
her head and expose the large dark eyes between their
long doll's lashes.

A stronger wave broke against the rock with a slapping
sound; a few drops from the cone of spray landed quite near
Mathias, carried by the wind. The salesman glanced anxiously at his suitcase, but the drops had not reached it. He

looked at his watch and immediately jumped up. It was five minutes after eleven; the forty-five minutes the garageman had stipulated were already past, the bicycle must be waiting for him. He climbed up the flat rocks, crossed the parapet by means of the little granite stairway, and hastened toward the square along the uneven cobbles of the quay, retracing his steps in the very direction he had taken when he had disembarked an hour before. The gumdrop-seller gave him a nod of recognition from the door of her shop as he passed.

As soon as he had turned the corner around the hardware store, he saw a shiny chromium-plated bicycle leaning against the movie bulletin-board behind the monument. The innumerable pieces of polished metal reflected the sunlight in every direction. As he approached Mathias could see what a fine model it was, furnished with every desirable accessory as well as with several others he did not recognize and therefore judged to be superfluous.

Walking around the bulletin-board, he entered the café–tobacco shop to pay for the use of the bicycle. No one was there, but a piece of paper was prominently displayed in the middle of the counter, hung on the lever of the soda-water siphon. He read: "Take the bicycle in front of the door and leave two hundred crowns deposit here. Thank you."

Even as he took the bills out of his wallet, Mathias was astonished by this way of doing things: since he was being trusted enough not to require someone to take his deposit from him, why should he have to leave one at all? It was an unnecessary test of his honesty. If he obeyed and then a thief happened along before the garageman, how could he prove he had ever left the money? On the other hand, it would be easy enough not to leave the money and claim that a thief *had* happened along. Doubtless there was no malefactor on the island, no one to be mistrusted. He slipped the two bills required under the siphon and went out again.

He was arranging the elastic around the bottoms of his trousers when he recognized the jovial voice: "Good-looking bicycle, isn't it?"

"That one, yes! Good enough . . ." approved Mathias.

His eyes swept down the movie advertisement. In view of the herculean build of the man in Renaissance costume, he would scarcely have much difficulty drawing toward him the upper part of the girl's body; he must have preferred keeping her in that position, bent backward—perhaps so that he could look into her face more easily. On the ground, at their feet, lying across the black and white tiles . . .

"That's last Sunday's program," interposed the garage-man. "I'm expecting the new poster in this morning's mail, with the reels."

Wanting to buy a pack of cigarettes, Mathias returned to the café for a minute with his interlocutor, who seemed quite surprised to discover the money for the deposit under the soda-water siphon; he protested that this formality was unnecessary, returned the two bills to Mathias, and crumpled into a ball the paper hanging from the siphon.

On the doorstep they exchanged a few insignificant words. The tobacconist again pointed out his bicycle's features: tires, brakes, gears, etc. Finally he wished the salesman good luck as the latter climbed onto the seat.

Mathias thanked him. "I'll be back by four," he said as he rode off. He held the handlebars in his right hand and in his left the little suitcase which he did not wish to attach to the luggage rack in order not to lose any more time than necessary at each stop. The suitcase was not very heavy and would not get in his way, for he did not expect to travel either acrobatically or at great speeds.

He headed across the uneven cobbles toward the plot of

ground surrounding the town hall. Then he took the road to
the left, toward the big lighthouse. As soon as he had left
the square, he traveled without the slightest difficulty, quite
satisfied with his vehicle.

The cottages on each side of the road already had the
typical look of those in the country: a single story with a
low door between two square windows. He would visit them
on the way back, if he had time; he had delayed far too
long—and to no purpose—in this town. He made a quick
calculation of how much time remained until the boat left:
barely five hours, from which he would have to subtract the
time taken by the intervals on the bicycle: one hour at the
most was enough to allow for a distance totaling no more
than ten miles (unless he was mistaken). Thus he had about
four hours at his disposal for sales (and refusals); that is,
two hundred forty minutes. He would not waste time insist-
ing at great length to recalcitrant customers: as soon as he
perceived their intention not to buy, he would pack up and
move on; in this way he would get through most refusals in
a few seconds. As for sales, he would have to count on an
average of ten minutes for each one, which would reasonably include brief expeditions on foot in the villages. On
this basis his two hundred forty minutes represented the
sale of twenty-four watches—perhaps not the most expensive
ones, but, for instance, the series at one hundred fifty or one
hundred seventy crowns, on an average, with a profit . . .

At the very moment he passed the town limits he remembered the sailor, his sister, and his three nieces. He happened
to be just in front of the last house, which was on the right-
hand side a little apart from the rest—so that without fla-
grantly cheating he could consider it as the first house outside town. He stopped his bicycle, leaned it against the wall,
and knocked against the wooden panel of the door.

He looked at his nails. A long streak of grease, still wet,

lined the inside of his fingers. Yet he had not touched the chain. He looked at the handlebars, passed his hand under the right-hand grip and over the brake lever; new spots appeared at the ends of his index and middle fingers. Probably the garageman had just greased the brake coupling and afterward had forgotten to wipe off the lever. Mathias was looking around for something to wipe his hands on when the door opened. He quickly concealed his hand in his pocket where it encountered the unopened pack of cigarettes, the bag of gumdrops, and last of all the wad of cord against which he rubbed the inside of his fingers as carefully as was possible in such haste, without the assistance of his other hand, and at the bottom of a full pocket.

The exchange of preliminary formulas followed at once—the brother working for the steamship company, the wrist watches at prices defying all competition, the hallway cutting the house down the middle, the first door to the right, the big kitchen, the oval table in the middle of the room (actually a dining room table), the oilcloth with the many-colored little flowers, the pressure of his fingers on the copper-plated clasp, the cover folding back, the black memorandum book, the prospectuses . . .

On the other side of the table, on the sideboard (a dining room sideboard, too), between various objects ranging from a coffee mill to a spiny tropical fish mounted on a board, was a rectangular, chromium-plated metal frame eight inches high, leaning on an invisible support; inside the frame was a photograph of Violet as a young girl.

It was not Violet, of course, but someone who looked very much like her—especially her face, for the clothes in the picture were those of a child, in spite of the nascent outlines of the body wearing them, which might already be a young woman's—in miniature. The subject was wearing her everyday clothes—those of a little peasant girl—which was surprising, since country people do not customarily have this kind of snapshot enlarged: photographs usually commemorate some event and are posed for in Sunday clothes (generally Communion dress, at such an age), between a chair and a potted palm in the photographer's studio. Violet, on the contrary, was standing against the rectilinear trunk of a pine tree, her head leaning against the bark, her legs braced and slightly spread, her hands clasped behind the small of her back. Her posture, an ambiguous mixture of surrender and constraint, made it look as if she might have been bound to the tree.

"That's a pretty girl you have there!" the salesman said good-naturedly.

"Don't mention her, she's a real curse. And don't be fooled by those obedient airs: she's got a devil inside her! A wild animal!"

The familiar conversation began; but Mathias realized that in spite of his interest in the girls' education—particularly in young Jacqueline's, whose disobedience caused so much trouble—even in spite of the pleasure he took in Maria's and Jeanne's splendid engagements, their mother had no intention of buying anything at all. The question of wedding presents for the two elder sisters had been settled long ago and all further expenses were now to be limited to what was strictly necessary.

Unfortunately the woman was garrulous, and he had to listen to interminable stories which were of no interest to him but which he dared not interrupt, now that he had imprudently introduced himself as a friend of the family. Thus he became acquainted with the exact circumstances of the two prospective sons-in-law, and with their plans as future husbands. After the honeymoon on the continent, one household would return to live on the island, while the other was to be established. . . . Violet's legs are spread, though

still in contact with the trunk—both heels touching the bark
at the roots, separated by half the circumference of the tree
(about sixteen inches). The cord holding them in that position cannot be distinguished because a clump of grass is
growing in front of the tree. Her forearms are bound together behind the small of her back, each hand in the crook
of the opposite elbow. Her shoulders must be attached to
the tree, too, probably under her armpits by means of
thongs, though it is difficult to see these. The child looks
exhausted and tense at the same time; her head is bent to the
right, in fact the whole body is slightly twisted in this direction, the right hip higher and projecting beyond the other,
only the front part of the right foot resting on the ground,
and the right elbow out of sight, although the other protrudes beyond the trunk. The snapshot, taken the previous
summer by a tourist visiting the island, is full of life in spite
of the slightly frozen pose. The stranger had stayed only
one day, fortunately, for God knows what would have happened with a man like that. The woman was of the opinion
that her daughter required severe discipline, for now that
she had had the misfortune to lose her husband (as the
salesman doubtless knew), the girl took advantage of it to
plague her poor mother out of her wits. She already was
dreading the moment when she would be without the two
older girls, who were so well-behaved, and left alone in the
house with this heartless child who at thirteen was a disgrace
to the whole family.

Mathias wondered what the girl could ever have done to
make her own mother speak of her with such hatred. Certainly she seemed precocious, but "heartless," "perverse,"
"wicked" . . . that was quite a different matter. The story
of the young fisherman whose engagement—it was claimed
—she had just ruined was rather vague. To say the least,
any young man actually "in love" with such a child was

playing rather an odd role in the first place. And why had the tourist sent his little companion of a single afternoon a photograph so expensively framed? The mother spoke unsmilingly of the girl's "magic power" and assured him that "not so long ago she would have been burned as a witch for less."

At the foot of the pine tree the dry grass began to blaze, as well as the hem of the cotton dress. Violet twisted at the waist and flung back her head, opening her mouth. Finally, however, Mathias succeeded in taking his leave. Yes, he would tell the overindulgent uncle about his Jacqueline's latest escapade. No, he wouldn't have a chance to meet her this morning because she was tending sheep at the edge of the cliff, far from the road, and even if he should leave the road it would be in the opposite direction—toward the Marek farm—unless he continued straight ahead to the lighthouse.

He avoided looking at his watch, anticipating his vain regrets at again having lost so much time. He tried instead to pedal faster, but the suitcase got in his way; he coasted in order to shift gears, holding the handlebars and the handle of the suitcase in his left hand—which was uncomfortable. The grade was steeper now, obliging him to slow down: besides, the sun and the heat were becoming excessive.

He stopped twice to visit isolated houses along the road; he was in such a hurry to leave them that he suspected he had spoiled the sales by not staying ten seconds longer.

When he reached the fork to the mill he continued straight ahead: the detour suddenly seemed futile.

A little farther on, with the excuse that it was too modestly built, he passed without stopping a cottage just off the road —which was level from now on. He thought he would make at least an appearance at the Marek farm: he had known the family for so long, certainly he would sell something there. The road to the farm forked left from the main road after the next bend; at the same point on the right would be the path to the southwest coast—where young Violet is tending sheep at the edge of the cliff . . .

The tide is still rising. The sea dashes forward all the more violently because of the inshore wind. After the big waves crash against the shore, a series of whitish cascades streams back down the smooth slope. Sheltered by the foremost rocks, reversed by the undertow, little flakes of rust-colored foam whirl about in the sunshine.

In a hollow to the right, the waves, more peaceful here, die out one after the other on the smooth sand, leaving thin traces of foam which advance in successive and irregular festoons—ceaselessly effaced and revived in ever-fresh designs.

He was at the crossroads already, and there was the white milestone (it was sixteen hundred yards to the big lighthouse at the end of the road).

The crossroads appeared immediately afterward: to the left the road to the farm, to the right a path that was quite broad at the outset but which subsequently narrowed to a vague dirt track—twisting to avoid roots and stumps, briar patches, and clumps of stunted gorse—just wide enough for the bicycle to pass. After a few hundred yards the ground sloped gently toward the first rises of the cliff. From here on Mathias could coast down.

II

A rectangular shadow less than a foot wide crossed the white dust of the road. It lay at a slight angle from the perpendicular without quite reaching the opposite side: its rounded—almost flat—extremity did not protrude beyond the middle of the road, of which the left side remained unshaded. Between this extremity and the close-cropped weeds bordering the road had been crushed the corpse of a little frog, its legs open, its arms crossed, forming a slightly darker gray spot on the dust of the road. The creature's body had lost all thickness, as if nothing but the skin were left—hard, dessicated, and henceforth invulnerable—clinging to the ground as closely as the shadow of an animal about to leap, limbs extended—but somehow immobilized in air. To the right the real shadow, which was much darker, gradually became paler, disappearing altogether after a few seconds. Mathias lifted his head toward the sky.

The upper edge of a cloud had just concealed the sun; a rapidly shifting bright fringe indicated its position from moment to moment. Other clouds, diffuse yet of less than ordinary size, had appeared here and there from the southwest. Most were of indeterminate shapes which the wind

75

broke up into loose meshes. Mathias followed the trajectory of a sitting frog which stretched out to become a bird seen in profile, wings folded, with a rather short neck, like that of the sea gull, and a slightly curved beak; even its big round eye was recognizable. For a fraction a second the giant gull seemed to be perched on top of the telegraph pole whose unbroken shadow extended once again across the road. In the white dust the shadows of the wires could not be distinguished.

A hundred yards beyond, a country woman carrying a knapsack was walking toward Mathias—doubtless coming from the village near the big lighthouse. The winding road and the situation of the crossroads at the bottom of a hill prevented her from seeing where the traveler had come from. He could just as well have come directly from the town as be returning from the Marek farm. On the other hand, the woman would have noticed this inexplicable stand-still, which he himself was surprised at, now that he thought about it. Why should he have stopped in the middle of the road, his eyes raised toward the clouds, holding in one hand the handlebars of a chromium-plated bicycle and in the other a small fiber suitcase? Only then did he sense the numbness he had been floating in (for how long?); he did not succeed in figuring out why, in particular, he had not gotten back onto the bicycle instead of pushing it along in this unhurried fashion, as if he had nothing better to do.

The country woman was now only fifty yards away from him. She was not looking at him but had certainly noticed his presence and his unusual behavior. It was too late to spring onto the seat and pretend to have been riding along ever since he had left the town, or the farm, or anywhere else. No hill, however small, had obliged him to walk the bicycle instead of riding it in this part of the country, and his dismounting could only be justified by an accident (not a serious one) that had occurred to some delicate part of the machinery—the gearshift, for instance.

He considered the rented bicycle gleaming in the sun, and decided that such slight disturbances sometimes occur in even the newest machines. Seizing the handlebars in his left hand, which was already holding the suitcase, he leaned over to inspect the chain. It seemed to be in perfect condition, carefully oiled, fitting satisfactorily around the gearing of the sprocket-wheel. Nevertheless, the traces of grease still clearly visible on his right hand proved that he had already been compelled to touch it as least once. However, this indication was quite useless: as soon as his right hand had actually brushed against the chain, the tips of all four fingers were blackened by several fresh grease spots which greatly exceeded the old ones in size and intensity—even partially concealed them. He added two horizontal stripes to the heel of his thumb, which had remained unspotted; then he straightened up. Two steps away he recognized the wizened, yellow face of old Madame Marek.

Mathias had arrived that very morning by the steamer, intending to spend the day on the island; he had immediately made efforts to procure a bicycle, but while waiting until one was available he had begun his rounds at the harbor, contrary to his original plans. Since he had not succeeded in selling any of his merchandise—notwithstanding its excellent quality and moderate price—he had doggedly called at all (at almost all) the houses along the road where his chances had seemed somewhat better. He had wasted still more time doing this—so much time that once back at the crossroads he had suddenly become alarmed at how late it had grown and had decided it would be wiser to continue straight ahead instead of making another detour all the way

to the farm. To add to his troubles, the gearshift of the
bicycle he had rented at the café–tobacco shop was not
working properly and . . .

The old woman was going to pass without speaking to
him. She had stared at him and then looked away as if she
did not know him. At first he felt a kind of relief, then
wondered if the contrary would not have been preferable.
Finally it occurred to him that perhaps she had pretended
not to recognize him on purpose, though he could not see
why she should show any reluctance to gossip with him for
a few minutes, or in any case to say good morning, if nothing
more. On the off chance, he decided to speak first, in spite
of the considerable effort it cost him at this particular moment. That way, at least, he would know how far he could
go. He emphasized the grimace he had begun, imagining it
resembled a smile.

But now it was too late to attract the woman's attention
by a mere change of expression. She had already passed
between the dried corpse of the frog and the rounded extremity of the telegraph pole. Soon she would be far behind
him, and it would take a human voice to keep her from
continuing toward still more inaccessible regions. Mathias
clenched his right hand around the polished metal of the
handlebars.

A sentence jolted out of his mouth—obscure and overlong,
too sudden to be altogether friendly, grammatically incor-
rect—in which he could make out, nevertheless, the essential
formulas: "Marek," "good morning," "not recognized." The
old woman turned toward him without understanding what
he had said. He managed to repeat the indispensable words
more calmly, completing them by giving his own name.

"Well, well!" the old woman said, "I didn't recognize you."

She thought he seemed tired, "funny-looking" was how
she put it. At the time of their last meeting, more than two

years ago (the last time she had been in town, at her son-in-law's), Mathias was still wearing his little mustache. . . . He protested: he had never worn a mustache, or a beard either. But the old woman did not seem convinced by his insistence. To change the subject, she asked him what he was doing so far from town: there wasn't much chance of his finding many electric appliances to repair—especially out here in the country where almost everyone used oil anyway.

Mathias explained that he was no longer an itinerant electrician. He was selling wrist watches these days. He had arrived on the steamer this very morning, and planned to spend the day. He had rented a bicycle, which unfortunately was not working so well as its owner had claimed it would. (He showed his grease-stained hand.) Besides, he had wasted so much time getting as far as the crossroads that when he . . .

Madame Marek interrupted him. "That's right, you wouldn't have found anyone at the house."

The salesman let her talk on. She told him about her daughter-in-law's departure for a fifteen-day trip to the mainland. And her eldest son would be in town all morning (the other two were sailors). Josephine had lunch at her family's on Tuesdays. Her grandchildren didn't come home from school until twelve-thirty, except the eldest boy, who worked as an apprentice at the bakery and didn't come home until evening. That boy wasn't all there: why only the week before . . .

Mathias might have met the father, or the son, for he had begun his rounds at the harbor, contrary to his original plans. Relying more on his country customers, he had then doggedly called at all the houses along the road. Here as in town he had wasted still more time. He hoped for a more favorable reception at the Marek's at least—he wouldn't have missed visiting his old friends for anything; he had been

disappointed to find the house closed and apparently empty;
he had been obliged to leave without news of the family—
of Madame Marek, her children, her grandchildren. He was
wondering what their absence—everyone's—could mean at
such an hour, when most people are at home eating dinner.
How could he help worrying over this incomprehensible
solitude?

His ears, straining for a clue, hear nothing; even his
breathing, that might break the silence, stops of its own
accord. Yet he cannot hear the slightest noise inside. No one
speaks. Nothing moves. Everything is dead still. Mathias
leans toward the closed door.

He knocks again, this time with his ring, on the door
panel which echoes as if he had struck an empty box; but
he already knows how futile such a gesture is: if someone
were at home the door would be open on a sunny day like
this, and probably the windows too. He lifts his head toward
those on the first floor; not a sign of life there either—shutter
pushed open, lifted curtain falling back, silhouette disappearing—not even that premonitory confusion of the gaping
window recesses where someone leaning out might have just
disappeared, or someone who has suddenly appeared is going to lean out.

Propping his bicycle against the wall, he takes a few undecided steps on the beaten earth floor of the courtyard.
He reaches the kitchen window and tries to look in, but it
is too dark inside to see anything. He turns back toward the
door by the same way he came into the courtyard, walks
two or three yards in that direction, stops, turns around and
walks in the opposite direction, glances again at the door
and at the closed shutters of the ground-floor windows, continuing this time as far as the garden fence. The lattice-gate
is locked too.

Returning to the house, he approaches what must be the

kitchen window and checks to see if the heavy wooden shutters are bolted or merely drawn: useless, in that case, trying to see anything inside.

He returns to where he left the bicycle. There is nothing else to do but leave.

He is very disappointed. Here, at least, he was hoping for a more favorable reception. All the way to the farm his spirits had been rising at the prospect of a visit to his old childhood friends, never suspecting they could all be away from home at once.

Ever since that morning—ever since the night before—his spirits had been rising at the prospect of a visit to his old childhood friends; he told himself how surprised they would be to see him—he had never revisited the island, and after all he had been born here. He had already seen Robert Marek's four children on several occasions, however, when they were spending their short vacations with their uncle in the city, only a few doors away from his own house. They must have grown since the last time, there was a good chance he might not even recognize them now, but he would make sure that their parents didn't notice that. Perhaps he would be invited to stay to lunch; that would certainly be more pleasant than gobbling down the two sandwiches he had brought along for a snack; the heat had turned them to jelly in the left pocket of his duffle coat.

The heat was certainly becoming excessive. And the road was growing steeper, obliging him to slow down. He stopped twice at isolated houses along the road. Realizing at once that he would sell nothing, he left them almost immediately. When he reached the fork to the mill, he continued straight ahead: his information about the people there left him no hope of selling even the cheapest of his wares; it was useless going there under such conditions; he had wasted enough time that way.

A little farther on he noticed a cottage set back from the road at the end of a long, ill-kept path. Its poverty-stricken appearance excused him from even attempting a visit there. He looked at his watch: it was after midday.

It was easier riding now that the road had stopped going uphill. Soon he was at the crossroads. On the white milestone he read the freshly repainted directions: "Black Rocks Lighthouse—One Mile." Everyone on the island called it "the big lighthouse." After another fifty yards he left the road, turning left on the fork to the Marek farm.

The countryside was noticeably different here: there was an embankment on either side of the road lined with a thick, virtually unbroken hedge behind which rose the occasional trunk of a pine leaning toward the southwest, the direction of the prevailing winds (that is, the trees on the left side of the drive leaning over the hedge, those on the right leaning away from it).

In his haste to reach his immediate goal, Mathias tried to pedal faster. The bicycle chain began to make an unpleasant sound—as if it were rubbing sideways against the sprocket-wheel. He had already felt something strange about it shifting gears on the last hill, but he had not given it any thought, and the grating noise had gradually diminished—unless he had merely ceased noticing it. Now, on the contrary, it grew more pronounced—so rapidly that the traveler decided to stop. He put his suitcase down on the road and crouched down to examine the transmission, turning the pedal with one hand. He decided that he needed only to apply a little pressure to the sprocket-wheel, but in manipulating it he brushed against the chain itself and covered his fingers with spots of grease which afterward he had to wipe off as well as he could on the weeds growing along the road. He got back onto the seat. The suspicious noise had virtually disappeared.

As soon as he had entered the courtyard of beaten earth that extended in front of the farmhouse (actually the terminal enlargement of the road which came to a dead end here), he saw that the heavy wooden shutters of both ground-floor windows were drawn. The door between them, which he expected to find wide open, was also closed. The two upper-floor windows, situated just over those on the ground floor, had their shutters open but were closed in spite of the bright sunshine on the panes. Between them, above the door, was a large expanse of gray stone where a third window seemed to be missing; instead a little niche had been cut into the wall, as if for a statuette; but the niche was empty.

On either side of the door was a clump of mahonia; the still-greenish flowers were beginning to turn yellow. Mathias propped his bicycle against the wall of the house under the drawn shutters of the first window, to the left of the left mahonia bush. He walked to the door, still holding his suitcase in his hand, and knocked on the door panel—for conscience' sake, since he knew that it would not be opened.

After a few seconds he knocked again, this time with his ring. Then he stepped back and lifted his head toward the first-floor windows. Obviously no one was there.

He looked toward the haysheds at the end of the courtyard, turned back toward the door by the same way he had entered the courtyard, walked three yards in that direction, stopped, turned around and walked in the opposite direction again, and continued this time as far as the garden fence. The lattice-gate was padlocked.

He returned to the house. The shutters of what must have been the kitchen window looked as if they had been merely pushed together to keep out the sunlight. He walked over and tried to open them, but did not succeed: the bolts had been shot inside.

Mathias could do nothing but leave. He returned to where he had propped the bicycle against the wall under the other window, got on it and took the same road back, holding the handlebars in his right hand and the suitcase in his left— which he also used to apply a slight pressure to the left grip of the handlebars. He had hardly reached the main road when the grinding noise began again—much louder this time. About a hundred yards in front of him a country woman carrying a knapsack was walking in his direction.

He would have to get off again in order to push the chain back onto the cogs of the sprocket-wheel. As before, he could not help dirtying his fingers. When the operation was completed and he stood up, he realized that the wizened, yellow-faced woman about to pass him was old Madame Marek.

She did not recognize him right away. If he had not spoken to her first, she would have gone on without looking at him, so little chance did she think there would be of meeting him here. To excuse herself she claimed that Mathias' face had changed since the last time they had seen each other, in the city, and that he looked very tired today —which was to be expected, since he had had to get up much earlier than usual to take the boat, and without having gone to bed earlier the night before. Besides, he hadn't been sleeping well for several days.

Their last meeting had been at least two years ago. Mathias announced that he had changed his job since then: he was selling wrist watches these days. He was disappointed to have found no one at the farm, for his moderately-priced wares would certainly have interested Robert and his wife. How did it happen that neither of them was at home, nor any of the children? Mathias hoped that they were all well, nevertheless.

Yes, they were all in good health. The grandmother speci-

fied the reason for the absence of each one in turn—the
father in town, the mother on the mainland for fifteen days,
the children not yet back from school, etc. . . . —and declared
that if Mathias passed by again in the course of the afternoon
he would find Robert at home, and Josephine as well; the
poor girl certainly needed a watch to get her work done on
time—she was always fifteen minutes late for something.

The salesman had doubtless just missed the father and
the three younger children who generally came home
around twelve-thirty. They took the short cut across the
fields and came in through the garden, behind the house.
Perhaps, she added, they had arrived by now; but she did
not invite Mathias to join her, which he dared not propose
himself, hesitating to disturb them all at dinnertime. She
merely asked him to let her see the watches and he had to
show them there at the roadside, putting the suitcase down
on the ground. Just next to it, flattened in the dust of the
road, was the dried corpse of a toad.

In a hurry to get home, the old woman did not take long
to decide. She wanted to give a nice present to her grandson
—the one who worked as an apprentice at the bakery—for
his seventeenth birthday. She took the hundred-fifty-crown
model (with metal strap)—that was good enough, she said,
for a boy. The salesman assured her she would not regret
her choice, but the old woman was not interested in a description of the item's qualities; she cut short his explanations and guarantees, paid him, thanked him, wished him
good luck, and hurried away. Not knowing where to put
the watch which the salesman, accustomed to home sales,
was not equipped to wrap very carefully, the old woman
had fastened it around her own wrist—but without setting
the hands at the correct time, although the watch was
wound.

Crouching in front of his suitcase, Mathias replaced the

cardboard strips, the prospectuses, the black canvas memorandum book, closed the cover, and fastened the clasp. He
looked more closely at the grayish spot on the white dust
of the road which he had first taken for the remains of a
frog. The hind legs were too short—it must have been a toad
(besides, it was always toads that got run over). Its death
could not have occurred earlier than the night before, for
the creature's body was not as dry as the dust made it look.
Near the head, which was distorted by being flattened, a
red ant was trying to find a scrap that was still usable.

The surrounding patch of road changed color. Mathias
raised his eyes toward the sky. Moving rapidly, a cloud half-
torn apart by the wind covered the sun again. The day was
gradually becoming overcast.

The salesman mounted his bicycle and continued on his
way. The air was growing cooler, the duffle coat more bear-
able. The ground neither rose nor fell; the good condition
of the road made riding easy. The wind blew from the left,
not impeding the bicyclist, who was pedaling rapidly, almost effortlessly, his little suitcase in one hand.

He made a stop at an isolated cottage at the edge of the
road—a simple one-story dwelling of the most ordinary kind.
Two clumps of mahonia framed the doorway, as in front of
most of the island's houses, and at the rear too. He leaned
his bicycle against the wall under the window and knocked
at the door panel.

The person answering the door appeared in its opening
at a much lower level than he had expected. It was doubtless
a child—height and size considered—even a rather young
child—but Mathias could not decide whether it was a boy
or a girl, for the silhouette quickly retreated into the shadow
of the hallway. He stepped in and closed the door behind
him. Because of the half-darkness to which his eyes had not

yet had time to grow accustomed, he did not know by what means the next door he passed through was opened.

A man and a woman were seated facing each other across a table. They were not eating; perhaps they had already finished. It looked as though they were expecting the salesman.

Mathias set down his suitcase on the unpatterned oilcloth. Taking advantage of their tacit consent, he unpacked his merchandise while delivering his sales-talk with some assurance. The two people sitting in their chairs listened politely; they even examined the strips of cardboard with a certain interest, passing them back and forth to each other and attempting one or two comments: "This is a practical shape," "This is a more elegant case," etc. . . . But they seemed to be thinking of something else—or of nothing at all—to be weary, distressed, chronically ill, or perhaps suffering from some tremendous disappointment; their comments were confined to scrupulously objective remarks: "This one is thinner," "The other has a convex glass," "Here's a rectangular face," . . . of which the obvious futility did not seem to disturb them.

Finally they decided on one of the cheapest models—one just like the one the old country woman had bought. They indicated their choice without enthusiasm, and as if without reason. ("Why wouldn't this one do just as well?") They exchanged no words with the salesman himself. It was as if they scarcely saw him. When the man had taken out his wallet and paid for the watch, Mathias regretted not having insisted on an item two or three times as expensive, thinking that they would have paid for it with no more hesitation, with the same indifference.

No one came to show him out. The new watch (with the metal strap) was still lying on the oilcloth between the woman and her already distracted companion: shiny, lost, unjustified.

There was not another house until the village at Black
Rocks. Mathias pedaled steadily for about two-thirds of a
mile. The bicycle cast only a pale—and intermittent—shadow
which soon disappeared altogether. Against the gray background of the sky, in which only a few vague blue spots
remained, rose the lighthouse, now quite near.

The structure was one of the highest of the countryside,
as well as one of the most massive. Besides the white-painted,
slightly conical tower itself, it included a semaphore, a radio
station, a small power-house, four enormous foghorns for
bad weather, and several accessory structures sheltering machines and equipment, as well as lodgings for the workmen
and their families. Had these employees been engineers or
even mechanics, they would have constituted a wealthy·
enough clientele for Mathias, but unfortunately the lighthouse workers were not the sort who bought their watches
from traveling salesmen.

There remained the village proper. Originally merely a
cluster of three or four farmhouses, it had grown with the
neighboring installations, although more modestly. Even had
Mathias' memory been better, he would scarcely have recognized it, so much had it developed since his childhood: perhaps ten cottages, jerry-built but of neat appearance, now
surrounded and concealed the original group, whose thicker
walls, lower roofs, and smaller windows were evidence of
their earlier date. The new constructions were not a part of
the world of wind and rain: although actually quite similar
to their predecessors—granted certain minor differences—
they seemed without climate, and at the same time without
history and geographical location. It was remarkable that
they managed to withstand, with apparently equal success,
the same raw weather as the others; unless atmospheric
conditions had grown somewhat gentler . . .

It was no different now from anywhere else. There was a

grocery and a café, of course, almost at the beginning of the village. Leaving his bicycle near the door, Mathias went in.

The arrangement inside was like that of all such establishments in the country or even in the suburbs of big cities —or on the quays of little fishing ports. The girl behind the bar had a timorous face and the ill-assured manners of a dog that had been ill-assured manners of a dog that had been ill-assured manners of a girl who served behind the. . . . Behind the bar, a fat woman with a satisfied, jovial face beneath her abundant gray hair was pouring drinks for two workmen in blue overalls. She handled the bottle with the sure gestures of a professional, raising the neck with a slight rotation of her wrist at the precise moment the liquid reached the edge of the glass. The salesman went to the bar, set his suitcase on the floor between his feet, and ordered an absinthe.

Without thinking, the salesman was about to order an absinthe when he changed his mind—just before having spoken the word. He cast about for the name of some other kind of drink, and, unable to think of any, pointed to the bottle the proprietress was still holding after having served the two lighthouse workers.

"I'll have the same," he said, and set the suitcase on the floor between his feet.

The woman put in front of him a glass like the first two; she filled it with her other hand, which had not yet released the bottle—making the same rapid movement, so that a large quantity of liquid was still in the air, between the bottom of the glass and the neck of the bottle, as she was already lifting the latter away. At the very second she had finished twisting her wrist, the surface of the poured liquid immobilized on a level with the edge of the glass—without the slightest miniscus—like a diagram representing the theoretical capacity of the glass.

Its color—rather dark reddish-brown—was that of the majority of wine-base apéritifs. Promptly returned to its place on the shelf, the bottle could not be distinguished from its neighbors in the row of different brands. Previously, when the woman had been holding it in her huge hand, the spread of the fingers—or else the position of the label in relation to the observer—had prevented him from determining its brand. Mathias wanted to reconstruct the scene in order to try to fasten on some fragment of bright-colored paper to compare with the labels lined up on the shelf. He succeeded only in discovering an anomaly which had not struck him at the time: the proprietress used her left hand to serve drinks.

He studied her more attentively as she rinsed and dried the glasses—with the same dexterity—but he could not establish a preliminary standard as to the respective functions of each hand in these complex operations; so that it was impossible for him to determine whether or not she was right- or left-handed. His mind grew so confused between what he saw with his own eyes and his recollection of the previous scene that he began to muddle right and left himself.

The woman put down her towel; she seized the coffee mill beside her, sat down on a stool, and began to turn the handle vigorously. In order not to tire either arm at such a speed, she ground the coffee with one arm and then the other alternately.

The coffee beans made a pattering noise as they were crushed in the gearing, and when one of the two men said something to his companion Mathias could not hear him clearly. Several syllables, however, took shape in his mind, resembling the word "cliff" and—less positively—the verb "to bind." He cocked his ears; but no one was speaking any longer.

The salesman found it strange that they had fallen silent in this way ever since he had come in, sipping their apéritifs and putting their glasses on the bar after each swallow. Perhaps he had disturbed them in the midst of an important conversation? He tried to imagine what it could be about. But suddenly he was afraid to guess, and dreaded the possibility that the subject might be broached again, as if their words, without their knowing it, might have concerned him. It would not be difficult to go a good deal further along this irrational course: the words "without their knowing it," for instance, were superfluous, for if his presence had caused them to fall silent—although they were not embarrassed to speak in front of the proprietress—it was obviously because they . . . because "he" . . . "In front of the proprietress," or rather, "with" her. And now they were pretending not to know one another. The woman stopped grinding only to refill the coffee mill. The workmen managed to keep another mouthful at the bottoms of their glasses. To all intents and purposes no one had anything to say; yet five minutes before he had seen through the window all three talking animatedly together.

The proprietress was about to pour another drink for the two men; they were wearing blue overalls, like most of the lighthouse workers. Mathias leaned his bicycle against the shopwindow, pushed open the glass door, stood against the bar next to the two workmen and ordered an apéritif. After having served him, the woman began grinding coffee. She was middle-aged, fat, imposing, self-assured. At this time of day there was no sailor in her establishment. The house in which her café was located had no upper floor. The sparkling water of the harbor could not be seen through the door.

Evidently no one had anything to say. The salesman turned toward the room. For a moment he was afraid it was all going to begin over again: three fishermen he had not noticed when he came in—a very young man and two older ones—were sitting over three glasses of red wine at one of

the back tables; just then the youngest began speaking—but
the noise of the coffee mill might have kept Mathias from
hearing the beginning of the conversation. He cocked his
ears. As usual, it was about the slump in crab sales. He
turned back to the bar to finish this unidentifiable reddish
drink.

His eyes met those of the proprietress; she had been watching him on the sly as she ground her coffee, while he himself
had been looking in the other direction. He lowered his eyes
to his glass, as if he had noticed nothing. To his left the two
workmen were looking straight ahead, toward the bottles
lined up on the shelf.

"You wouldn't happen to be the man selling watches?"
the woman asked suddenly, her voice calm.

He lifted his head. She was still turning the handle of her
coffee mill, still staring at him—but kindly, he thought.

"Yes, I am," answered Mathias. "Someone must have told
you a salesman was coming this way. News travels fast
around here!"

"Maria, one of the Leduc girls, came in here just ahead of
you. She was looking for her sister, the youngest one. You
visited them this morning: the last house as you leave town."

"Yes, of course I visited Madame Leduc. Her brother is
a friend of mine—Joseph—the one who works for the steamship line. But I haven't seen the girls today, not one of them.
No one told me the youngest was here."

"She wasn't. Her mother sent her to tend the sheep. And
she ran away again. Always running off where she shouldn't,
making trouble somewhere."

"They send her as far as this with the sheep?"

"No, of course not: back there, under the crossroads.
Maria went to tell her to come home early, but no one was
there—only the sheep. The girl had picketed them in a
hollow."

Mathias shrugged, hesitating between amusement and compassion. The proprietress didn't take the matter too much to heart, but on the other hand she wasn't laughing either; her expression was completely neutral—certain of what she was talking about, yet attaching no importance to it—a vaguely professional smile on her lips, as if she were merely talking about the weather.

"It sounds as if she's something of a problem," the salesman said.

"A real devil! Her sister came all the way here on her bicycle to see if anyone knew where she was. If she doesn't take her home with her, there's going to be trouble."

"Children are a lot of trouble," said the salesman.

They were obliged to speak very loudly, in order to be heard over the noise of the coffee mill. Between sentences, the pattering noise of the coffee beans as they were crushed in the gearing was all that could be heard. To reach the village at Black Rocks, Maria must have passed Mathias on the road while he was visiting the exhausted-looking couple. Before that, to cross the moor between the road and the place where the sheep were grazing on top of the cliff, she couldn't have taken the same path he used, but a short cut probably, a short cut starting at the crossroads. In fact, the girl needed a certain amount of time to make the trip from the road to the cliff top and back and to look around a little as well. This amount of time would be much more than the few minutes it had taken the salesman to sell the one watch in the only house he had stopped at between the fork to the Marek farm and the village. And the distance between this fork and the cottage in question could not account for the difference either: beside the fact that it was scarcely more than five or six hundred yards, it was still the road both of them must have taken.

Thus Maria was already riding toward the cliff before he

himself had climbed back onto his own bicycle. Consequently, if she had taken the path opposite the fork to the Marek farm, she would have come upon the salesman in the middle of the road, gossiping with the old woman —or examining his bicycle chain, the clouds, the dead toad—for this prolonged stop had occurred within sight of the crossing—not two steps away from it, so to speak. (This same hypothesis—in which the girl used the same path Mathias had taken, to reach the cliff top—worked no better if presuming she had arrived at the cliff top before he had made his stop, since then she would have encountered the salesman on the path itself.)

She must have come by another road. But why had she mentioned him to the proprietress? Because of the rolling ground, it seemed unlikely—it was impossible—it was impossible—it was impossible that she had seen him from another path, supposing that she had been going toward the cliff top and he returning from it. Back there, in the sheltered hollow where the sheep were grazing, she had doubtless just missed him. After a rapid exploration of the environs, repeated calls, a few seconds' hesitation, she had returned to the main road—this time, probably, by the same path he had taken (the only one he knew), but the tire tracks were too numerous and too indistinct to be able to tell one from another. It seemed unlikely that there would be a new short cut between the sheep and the village at Black Rocks —not a very useful short cut in any case, given the size of the bay jutting into the land northwest of the lighthouse.

Mathias, who had omitted this last possibility in the course of all his previous deductions, feared for a moment that he might have to reconstruct his entire train of thought. But on reflection, he decided that even if this unlikely short cut had existed, it would not have been sufficient to negate the conclusions he had arrived at—although it would have modified his reasoning, without a doubt.

"I came in here as soon as I reached the village. If Maria was here shortly before, she must have passed me without my seeing her—while I was visiting customers: in the cottage along the road, the only one between the village and the crossroads. Before stopping there, I had gone to see my old friends the Mareks—where I waited for a long time in the courtyard: no one was there and I didn't want to leave without saying hello, hearing the family news, gossiping a little about the neighbors. I was born here on the island, you know. Robert Marek was a childhood playmate of mine. He had gone into town this morning. His mother—still an active woman—was marketing here at Black Rocks. Maybe you ran into her while she was here. Luckily I met her on her way back, at the crossroads—at the fork, I mean—but there is a crossroads there, since the road to their farm crosses the main road and continues as a path over the moor. If Maria went that way, she must have been there while I was waiting at the farmhouse. Didn't you say that the path just after the crossroads led to the cliff top—to that place on the cliff top where she took the sheep to graze?"

He had better stop. These specifications as to time and itinerary—both furnished and requested—were futile, suspect even—worse still: confusing. Besides, the fat woman had never said Maria took the road passing through the crossroads, but only that the Leduc sheep were grazing "after the crossroads"—an ambiguous expression, since it was impossible to know if she meant "after" in relation to her own village or to the town where Madame Leduc lived.

The proprietress did not answer his question. She was no longer looking at the salesman. Mathias thought he had not made himself heard above the noise of the coffee mill. He did not try again, however, and pretended to drink the liquid remaining in his glass. Afterward, he doubted whether he had spoken aloud at all.

He was glad of it: if it was useless to go over the details of his alibis with listeners as inattentive as this, it could only be dangerous to falsify those parts of his story relating to the sister, who would certainly remember which road she had taken. Doubtless she had reached the cliff top by another road—a short cut the proprietress must know about. It was stupid, under such conditions, to refer to the "fact" that the girl had taken a path at the crossroads.

Then the salesman remembered that the fat woman had not said "after the crossroads," but something like "under the crossroads"—which meant nothing in particular—or even nothing at all. As a last resource, there still remained. . . .

He had to make a conscious mental effort to understand that here too any attempt at deception would be useless: the place where the sheep were picketed had been determined beyond all possibility of dispute. They were always pastured in the one spot, perhaps, and Maria went there often. In any case, she had had time today, certainly, to examine the place as much as she liked. Furthermore: the sheep, left where they had been picketed, would be the most irrefutable indication of all. And besides, Mathias knew the hollow on the cliff top as well as anyone else. He would obviously not succeed in changing its position by pretending to interpret incorrectly the declarations of an indirect witness.

Anyway these various pieces of information concerning location and route were of no importance whatever. The thing to remember was that Maria could not have seen him crossing the moor, or else he would have seen her himself, especially since they were going in opposite directions. All these explanations were intended solely to account for the fact that they had not met each other when he stopped in the middle of the main road, near the toad's dried corpse —a place where such a meeting would be of no importance. To try to prove in addition that they had not seen each other because he was waiting at the Marek farm during that time would lead to nothing.

It would be much more likely, everyone would think, that Maria Leduc had passed the salesman well before he reached the crossroads, while he was showing his merchandise in another house—the mill, for instance. The few minutes Mathias had spent at the Marek farm, added to the trip to the cliff top and back on the little path, did not leave the girl time enough to look for her youngest sister in all the nooks and crannies of the cliff.

True enough, Mathias had not gone to the farm—but a conversation with the old woman at the crossroads sounded as if it would have lasted an even shorter time. The mill would be a solution less open to dispute. Unfortunately it too had to be rejected as altogether spurious for at least two reasons, one being that the salesman had no more made this side-trip to the mill than he had made the other to the farm.

As for the other reason, it must be confessed that Maria's investigations represented only the time it would take to sell a watch—near a crossroads—to repair a new bicycle, to tell the difference between a frog's skin and a toad's, to rediscover in the all-too-changeable shapes of clouds the fixed eye of a sea gull, to follow the movements of an ant's antennae in the dust.

Mathias prepared to recapitulate his movements since he had left the café–tobacco shop–garage on the rented bicycle. That had been at eleven-ten or eleven-fifteen. To establish the subsequent chronology of his stops presented no particular difficulty; but this would not be true in determining their respective lengths, which he had neglected to note. And the length of time on the road between each stop scarcely influenced his calculations, the distance from town to light-house not exceeding three miles—that is, scarcely more than fifteen minutes in all.

To begin with, the distance to the first stop being virtually negligible, he could state that the latter had occurred at exactly eleven-fifteen.

It was the last house as he left town. Madame Leduc had opened the door almost at once. The preliminaries had gone very fast: the brother working for the steamship line, the wrist watches at prices defying all competition, the hallway splitting the house down the middle, the door to the right, the big kitchen, the oval table in the middle of the room, the oilcloth with the many-colored little flowers, the pressure of his fingers on the suitcase clasp, the cover opening back, the black memorandum book, the prospec-tuses, the rectangular frame on top of the sideboard, the shiny metal support, the photograph, the sloping path, the hollow on the cliff sheltered from the wind, secret, calm, isolated as if by thick walls . . . as if by thick walls . . . the oval table in the middle of the room, the oilcloth with the many-colored little flowers, the pressure of his fingers on the suitcase clasp, the cover opening back as if on a spring, the black memorandum book, the prospectuses, the shiny metal frame, the photograph showing . . . the photograph showing the photograph, the photograph, the photograph, the photo-graph . . .

The noise of the coffee mill suddenly stopped. The woman rose from her stool. Mathias pretended to drink the liquid remaining in his glass. To his left, one of the workmen said something to his companion. The salesman cocked his ears; but again, no one was speaking any longer.

There had been the word "soup" at the end of a rather short sentence; perhaps the words "come home" as well.

It must have been something like ". . . come home in time for soup," beginning with words like "Be sure to . . ." or "I always . . ." It was just a figure of speech, probably; it had been several generations since the fishermen took soup at the noon meal. The woman seized the empty glasses before the two men, plunged them into the sink, washed them quickly, rinsed them under the tap, and set them upside down on the drainboard. The man next to Mathias thrust his right hand into his trouser pocket and brought out a handful of coins.

"We're going to be late for soup again," he said, counting out the money on the tin slab that covered the bar.

For the first time since he had left town, the salesman looked at his watch—it was after one—one-seven, exactly. He had already been on the island over three hours—three hours and one minute. And he had sold only two wrist watches, both at one hundred fifty crowns.

"I'll have to hurry," said the second workman, "on account of the kids going to school."

The proprietress picked up the money with a quick movement of her hand, smiled, and said "Thank you, gentlemen!" She put the coffee mill in a cupboard. She had not emptied the tray after having ground the beans.

"Yes, children are a lot of trouble," Mathias repeated.

The two lighthouse employees had left. He thought, too late, that he should have tried to sell them watches. But he still had to obtain information on two points: where was Maria Leduc going after she left Black Rocks? Why had she mentioned him? He tried to find some expression that would give an air of indifference to the question.

"And sometimes satisfaction, too," the fat woman said.

The salesman nodded. "Of course they are!" And, after a pause, "One man's trouble . . ." he began.

He went no further. That was not at all the right formula.

"Maria went home," the woman continued, "by the path along the cliff."

"That's no short cut," Mathias declared, hoping to find out if it was.

"It's a short cut if you're walking; but with her bicycle, she'll take longer that way than by the road. She wanted to see if Jacqueline would be playing down on the rocks, near Devil's Hole."

"Maybe she wasn't that far away. She might not have heard Maria on account of the wind. They'll find her peacefully tending her sheep in the usual place, like a good girl."

A good girl. Peaceful, in the quiet hollow.

"Then too," said the woman, "they may find her still prowling around here—over at the lighthouse. And maybe not alone either. At thirteen, it's hard to believe."

"Bah! She can't do anything very bad. . . . She wasn't going to play too close to the edge, was she—where the rocks are dangerous? Sometimes it caves in in places. You have to watch where you put your feet."

"Don't worry about that. She's a lively one!"

Lively. She was. Lively. Alive. Burned alive.

"Anyone can lose his footing," the salesman said.

He took his wallet from the inside pocket of his jacket and removed a ten-crown note from it. He took advantage of this movement to put back in place a newspaper clipping that stuck out a little beyond the other papers. Then he held out the note to the proprietress. When she gave him his change, he noticed that she put the coins on the counter, one by one, with her left hand.

Then she picked up his glass which rapidly underwent the series of ablutionary operations: sink, circular rubbing, tap, drainboard. Now the three identical glasses were again lined up on the drainboard—as they had been on top of the bar—but at a noticeably lower level this time, and nearer

one another besides, empty (that is, transparent and colorless instead of opaque because of the brown liquid which
had filled them so perfectly), and upside down. Nevertheless, the shape of these glasses—a cylinder bulging at the
middle—made their silhouettes virtually the same whether
they were standing rightside up or on their rims.

Mathias' situation was unchanged. Neither his own reasoning nor the proprietress' words had enlightened him on the
essential point: why had Maria Leduc just mentioned his
presence on the island apropos of her sister's disappearance?
That was the one thing to find out, and he would scarcely
further his knowledge on the point by disputing the existence
of more or less favorable short cuts in the inextricable
tangle of paths that ran along the cliff top in all directions.

Why would the girl have mentioned him, unless she had
seen him riding over the moor—"under the crossroads"—
where there was no reason for him to be? The fact that he
had not seen her was all too easy to explain. Their two
paths, separated from each other by the considerable unevenness of the ground, had only a few privileged points
from which two observers could see each other at the same
time. At a given moment he and the girl had occupied these
favorable positions, but she alone had turned in his direction,
so that the reciprocity of their points of view had not func-
tioned. At that particular moment Mathias had his eyes
somewhere else—on the ground, for instance, or raised toward the sky, or looking in any direction except the right
one.

The girl, on the contrary, had immediately identified the
person she had glimpsed by the shiny bicycle and the little
brown suitcase her mother had just described to her. There
was no possibility of a mistake. Now she was hoping he
might know where her sister was hiding, for he seemed to
be coming back from where she was supposed to be. And

if there was a chance that the mother had related the salesman's remarks about his itinerary incorrectly, Maria might
even have been positive that he was coming back from the
cliff top. And in fact he remembered that while he had
been trying to leave the overly talkative Madame Leduc
without being actually rude, she had spoken of an eventual
meeting between him and her youngest daughter. The idea
was a preposterous one, of course. What would he be doing
on that awkward path without any houses along it and
leading nowhere?—except to the sea, to steep rocks, to a
hollow sheltered from the wind, and five sheep grazing on
their pickets under the superfluous vigilance of a thirteen-
year-old child.

He had recognized Violet immediately, she was wearing
the same peasant-girl disguise she had in the photograph.
Her thin black cotton dress was more suitable for mid-
summer, but it was so warm at the bottom of the hollow
that it seemed like August. Violet was there on the sunny
grass, half-sitting, half-kneeling, her legs bent under her,
the rest of her body vertical and slightly twisted toward
the right in a rather strained attitude. Her right ankle and
foot protruded from under the top of her thigh; the other
leg remained completely invisible below the knee. Her arms
were lifted, her elbows bent, and her hands were at the nape
of her neck—as if arranging her hair behind her head. A
gray sweater was lying next to her on the ground. The
sleeveless dress exposed the hollows of her armpits.

Turned toward him, she had not moved as he approached,
her eyes wide as they met his. But on reflection Mathias
wondered whether she was looking at him or at something
behind him—something of enormous size. Her pupils remained fixed; not a feature of her face moved. Without
lowering her eyelids or shifting her uncomfortable position,
she twisted the upper part of her body to the left.

He had to say something at any cost. The three glasses on the drainboard were nearly dry. The woman picked them up one after another and gave them a quick wipe of her towel; they disappeared under the counter from where she had originally taken them. They were lined up again at the end of a long row of others—all invisible to customers standing at the counter.

But arrangement by rows being impractical for serving, they were grouped in rectangles on the shelves: the three apéritif glasses had just been set down next to three similar glasses, ending a first series of six. A second identical series was just behind, then a third, a fourth, etc. . . . The sequence disappeared in the darkness at the back of the cupboard. To the right and to the left of this series, and on the shelves above and below it as well, were arranged other rectangular series of glasses: they varied in shape and size, rarely in color.

Nevertheless, certain differences of detail were noticeable. One glass was missing from the last row of those used for the wine-base apéritifs; two other glasses, furthermore, were not of the same make as the rest, from which they could be distinguished by a slight pinkish cast. This heterogeneous row thus included (from west to east): three units of the orthodox type, two pinkish glasses, and an empty place. In this series the shape of the glasses resembled a slightly convex barrel on a smaller scale.

It was from one of these—a colorless one—that the salesman had just drunk.

He lifted his eyes toward the gray-haired fat woman and saw that she was watching him—had been watching him, perhaps, for a long time now.

"Well, Maria. . . . What did she want me for? You said just now. . . . What did she mention me for?"

The proprietress continued to stare at him. She waited almost a minute before answering.

"No reason. She only wanted to know if anyone had seen you. She expected to find you in the village. That's part of the reason she came this far."

After another pause, she added: "I think she wanted to have a look at your watches."

"So that's what's at the bottom of it!" said the salesman. "Well, you're going to see for yourself that what I have here is well worth going a few miles out of your way to find. Her mother must have told her. If you ever admired splendid watches, ladies and gentlemen, prepare yourselves . . ."

As he continued in a tone bordering on parody, Mathias picked up his suitcase from between his feet and turned around to set it down on a table near the one where the three sailors were drinking. They looked in his direction; one moved his chair to be able to see better; the woman walked around the bar and came closer.

The copper-plated clasp, the cover, the black memorandum book, everything went as usual, without deviation or obstruction. Words, as always, worked a little less well than gestures, but with nothing too disturbing in the total effect. The proprietress wanted to try on several styles which had to be detached from the cardboard strips and afterward replaced as well as possible. She fastened them on her wrist one after another, moving her hand about in all directions to determine their effect, suddenly revealing a coquettish self-interest which her appearance scarcely suggested. She finally decided on a large watch with a heavily ornamented case in which the hours were indicated by tiny, complicated designs of interlaced knots rather than by numbers. Originally, perhaps, the artist had been inspired by the shapes of the twelve numbers; so little of them remained, however, that it was virtually impossible to tell the time—without a close examination, in any case.

Two of the sailors, who wanted their wives' advice, asked the salesman to stop by after lunch. They lived in the village, of which the topography could scarcely be complicated; nevertheless, they began extremely lengthy explanations to indicate the location of their respective dwellings. They probably gave him a number of useless or redundant details, but with such exactitude and such insistence that Mathias was completely confused. A description of the place containing willful errors would not have misled him more; he was not certain, in fact, that a good many contradictions were not mixed in with their redundancies. Several times he even had the impression that one of the two men was using the words "to the right" and "to the left" almost by chance—indiscriminately. A quick sketch of the cluster of houses would have cleared up everything; unfortunately, none of the sailors had anything to write with, the woman was too absorbed by her recent purchase to offer them a sheet of paper, and the salesman had no desire to have his memorandum book used as a spot-map. Since he intended to visit every house in the village anyway, he soon decided merely to nod with an understanding expression and not even listen to the rest of the directions, which he nevertheless punctuated now and then with a convincing "All right" or "Yes."

Since their two houses were in the same direction in relation to the café, the sailors had at first taken turns telling him where they were, the one who lived farthest away beginning his account where his companion left off. As an extra precaution, the first sailor began all over again as soon as the second one had finished. The successive versions referring to the same ground to be covered naturally included variations—which seemed, in fact, considerable. But then a real disagreement arose about the beginning of the route, and both men began to talk at once, each trying to impose his own point of view, although Mathias could not even understand the difference between them. The dispute would have been endless if the dinner hour had not forced them to put a provisional end to it: the salesman would settle the discussion later by telling them which way he considered better; since he spent his life on the road, he must be a specialist in such matters.

They paid for their wine and left, accompanied by the third, still silent, sailor. Mathias, who could not call on his customers before one-forty-five or two (because of the island's appreciably later daily routine as compared to that of the mainland), had plenty of time to eat his two sandwiches. He carefully put back the contents of his suitcase, closed it, and sat down at a table to wait for the return of the proprietress, who had disappeared into the room behind the counter; then he would order something to drink.

Alone now, he looked straight ahead, through the window, at the road that passed through the village. It was very wide, dusty—and empty. On the other side rose an unbroken stone wall higher than a man, doubtless screening some of the lighthouse outbuildings. He closed his eyes and thought how tired he was. He had risen early in order not to miss the boat. There was no bus line between his house and the harbor. In an alley of the Saint-Jacques district a ground-floor window revealed a deep, rather dark room; although it was already broad daylight, the light from a little lamp fell on the unmade bedsheets at the head of the bed; lit at an angle, from below, a lifted arm cast its magnified shadow on the wall and the ceiling. But he couldn't afford to miss the boat: this day on the island could save everything. Counting the first watch he had already sold in town this morning, just before getting on board, his sales still amounted

to no more than four. He would write them down later in
the memorandum book. He thought how tired he was.
Nothing disturbed the silence, neither in the café nor outside. No. On the contrary—in spite of the distance and the
closed door—the steady crashing of the waves against the
rocks beyond the lighthouse was distinctly audible. The
sound was so clear he was surprised he had not noticed it
sooner.

He opened his eyes. The sea, of course, was not visible
from here. A fisherman was standing behind the window
and looking into the café—one hand on the doorknob, the
other holding an empty bottle. Mathias thought it was one
of the men who had been in the café—the one who had not
spoken. But when the man came inside, the salesman saw
that he was mistaken. He realized, furthermore, that the
delighted expression on the newcomer's face was the result
of his own presence. The sailor walked straight over to him
with loud exclamations: "It's really you? I'm not seeing
things?"

Mathias rose from his chair in order to shake the hand
held out to him. He made the handclasp as brief as possible
and made a fist as he drew back his arm, so that his nails
were hidden within his palm.

"Oh yes, it's me all right."

"Good old Mathias. It's been a hell of a long time!"

The salesman fell back into his chair. He did not know
what to do. At first he had suspected a hoax: the fellow was
merely pretending to know him. Since he did not see the
fisherman's advantage in such a trick, he abandoned the
idea and declared without further reserve: "My God, yes!
It has been a hell of a long time!"

At this moment the fat woman returned; Mathias was not
sorry to have an opportunity to prove he was not a stranger,
that he really had friends on the island, that he could be

trusted. The sailor took her for his witness: "I come in here to buy some wine, and who do I find myself next to but old Mathias—I haven't seen him in I don't know how long. That's a good one!"

The salesman didn't know how long either; he too found the encounter strange. But it was useless trying to stir up his memories, he didn't even know what he should be looking for.

"Such things happen," the proprietress said.

She took the empty bottle and brought a full one in its place. After taking it from her, the sailor declared that it would be "best" to put it on his bill "with the others." The woman made a dissatisfied face, but did not raise any objection. Looking at the wall with a vague expression, the sailor then announced that with a second bottle he could invite "this old Matt" to lunch. He addressed himself to no one in particular. No one answered.

Doubtless it was up to Mathias to intervene. But the man turned to him and began to question him with an increased cordiality about what had become of him "since old times." It seemed difficult to tell him without knowing beforehand how long ago he meant. The salesman did not have to puzzle about this for long, however, for the sailor had apparently no intention of listening to his answer. His new old comrade spoke more and more rapidly, making gestures of which the vigor and extent endangered the full bottle in his left hand. Mathias soon gave up trying to unravel any clues concerning the common past supposedly linking him to this person. His entire attention barely sufficed to follow the movements—sometimes divergent, sometimes convergent, sometimes without apparent relation—of the free hand and the bottle of red wine. The former, more agile, led on the other; by weighing it down with a load equal to the one already encumbering the left hand, the agitation of both might have been reduced to almost nothing—to slight movements, slower and more orderly, less extensive, necessary perhaps, easy to follow, in any case, for an attentive observer.

But first of all there would have to be a certain lull to interrupt this series of intertwined gestures and sentences which increased from moment to moment, assuming an alarming intensity. The slight breaks still evident here and there were of no use, for they could only be discerned at a distance, hence too late, when the current was already re-established. Mathias regretted not having bought the second bottle when the occasion had obviously permitted. To return to that point now demanded an immediacy of reaction utterly beyond his power. He closed his eyes. Behind the sailor, the threatening—or liberating—wine, the glass door, the road, the stone wall, the sea continued to dash against the cliff in regular assaults. After the shock of each wave against the irregular rock walls came the sound of water falling back in a mass, followed by the rustling of innumerable white cascades streaming out of the hollows and down the projections of the rock, the diminishing murmur lasting until the next wave.

The sun had completely disappeared. Past the shoreline the sea appeared a flat, even green, opaque, as if it had been frozen. The waves seemed to form at a very short distance from land, suddenly swelling up, submerging the giant rocks off the coast and spreading milky fans behind them as they advanced, collapsing farther inshore, boiling into the indentations in the slope, surging into unsuspected holes, breaking against other waves in gutters and grottoes, or leaping toward the sky in plumes of surprising height—which nevertheless were repeated at the same points with each wave.

In an indentation protected by an oblique ledge, where

the calmer water lapped in rhythm with the undertow, a
thick layer of yellowish moss had accumulated, from which
the wind tore off long strips, spreading them in whorls along
the face of the cliff. Mathias was walking rapidly along the
path on the cliff top, his suitcase in one hand and his duffle
coat buttoned up, several yards behind the fisherman. The
latter, a full bottle dangling at the end of each arm, had
finally stopped talking because of the racket the waves
made. From time to time he turned around to face the
salesman, and cried out a few words, accompanying them
with confused movements of his elbows—vestiges of vaster
demonstrations. Mathias could not reconstitute their full
development, for he was obliged, in order to turn his ear
in the man's direction, to keep his eyes elsewhere. He
stopped for a moment in order to hear better. At the angle
of a narrow passageway between two almost vertical walls,
the water alternately swelled and hollowed with each
wave; at this point there was neither foam nor backwash;
the moving mass of water remained smooth and blue, rising
and falling against the rock walls. The disposition of the
nearby rocks forced a sudden influx of liquid into the
narrows so that the level rose to a height greatly exceeding
that of the initial wave. The collapse followed at once,
creating in a few seconds, in the same place, a depression
so deep that it was surprising not to be able to see sand,
or pebbles, or the undulating fronds of seaweed at the
bottom. On the contrary, the surface remained the same
intense blue tinged with violet along the rock wall. But
away from the coast, the sea appeared beneath a sky filled
with clouds, a flat, even green, opaque, as if it had been
frozen.

A reef farther offshore, where the swell seemed almost
insignificant, escaped the periodic immersion despite its low
configuration. A border of foam traced its contours. Three

gulls sat perfectly still on slight eminences on it, one a little
above the other two. They were sitting in profile, from
where he was standing, all three facing the same direction
and as identical as if they had been painted on canvas with
a stencil—legs stiff, body horizontal, head raised, eye fixed,
beak pointing toward the horizon.

Then the path descended to a little beach forming the
end of a narrow cove full of reeds. The triangle of sand was
completely covered by a beached fishing-smack and five or
six crab traps—big round openwork baskets made of thin
wands tied in place with osier knots. Immediately behind
the beach, near the first reeds, stood a lone cottage in the
center of a tiny lawn joined to the beach by a steep path.
The fisherman pointed one of the bottles toward the slate
roof and said, "Here we are."

Mathias was surprised by his voice, which had suddenly
become normal again: he no longer needed to shout to make
himself heard; the deafening noise of sea and wind had
disappeared so completely that it seemed he had been
transported several miles away. He looked behind him. The
slope down had barely begun, but the narrowness of the
cove and the hillocks along the cliff top above him were
enough to shelter the path almost immediately. The waves
were no longer visible—neither their successive arrivals, nor
their collapse, nor even their highest columns of spray—
concealed as they were by the rocky projections three-
quarters of the way across the entrance to this little basin.
Protected as if by a series of staggered dikes, the water here
had the smoothness of a flat calm. Mathias leaned over the
perpendicular edge.

He saw beneath him, barely above the surface, a horizontal platform roughly hewn from the rock, long enough
and wide enough for a man to stretch out comfortably.
Whether the formation was entirely natural or the result

of human handiwork, human beings certainly used it—or had used it in the past—probably for landing little fishing boats when the tide permitted. It was accessible, without too much difficulty, from the path, thanks to a series of breaks and faults forming a staircase missing only a few steps. The appointments of this rudimentary quay had been completed by four iron rings set into the vertical flank: the first two were quite low, on a level with the platform, about a yard apart, the others at a man's height, and a little wider apart. The unusual position in which the legs and arms were thus held revealed the body's grace. The salesman had recognized Violet immediately.

The likeness was perfect. It was not only the still-childish face with the huge eyes, the slender, round neck, the golden color of the hair, but even the same dimple near the armpits and the same fragile texture of the skin. Slightly below the right hip was a tiny blackish-red mole about the size of an ant and shaped like a three-pointed star—it looked very much like a v or a y.

The sun was hot down in this sheltered hollow. Mathias unbuckled the belt of his duffle coat; although the sky was overcast, the air did not seem so fresh now that the wind no longer reached him. Toward the open sea, on the other side of the reefs protecting the cove, the same low rock could still be seen with its fringe of foam and its three motionless gulls. They had not changed direction; but since they were rather far away they continued, despite the observer's change of position, to be seen from the same angle—that is, exactly in profile. Through an invisible opening in the clouds a pale sunbeam illuminated the scene with a wan, flat light. The rather lusterless white of the birds, in this light, gave an impression of distance that was impossible to estimate; the imagination might locate them at a mile off, or twenty feet, or even, without much more effort, within arm's reach.

"Here we are," said the fisherman boisterously. The sunbeam disappeared. The grayish plumage of the gulls was restored to its sixty yards' distance. At the edge of the steep cliff—too near, in places, following the recent cave-ins—the path sloped steeply down to the cottage and the bit of lawn. The cottage had only one small, square window. The roof was covered with thick, irregular, hand-hewn slates. "Here we are," the voice repeated.

They went in, the sailor followed by the salesman who closed the door behind him; the latch caught by itself. The cottage was really a good way from the village and not "thirty seconds" as its owner had promised. The latter's name was written on the door in chalk: Jean Robin. The clumsy script, both laborious and uncertain, suggested the school exercises of young children; but a child could not have reached so high on the door panel, even standing on tiptoe. The vertical side of the *b*, instead of being straight, leaned backward, and its upper loop, too rounded, looked like the reversed image of the bulge against which it was braced. Mathias, groping his way forward in the dark vestibule, wondered if the sailor had written these two words himself—and with what purpose. "Jean Robin"—the name suggested something, but nothing precise enough for him to locate the man in the past from which he claimed to emerge. The cottage's dark interior seemed more complicated than its size and its single window had led him to suppose from outside. The salesman directed his steps according to the back preceding him—turning several times at sharp angles—without discovering whether he was crossing rooms, hallways, or only going through doors.

"Be careful here," the man said, "there's a step."

His voice was low now, whispering, as if fearful of waking a sleeper, an invalid, an unfriendly dog.

The room impressed Mathias as being rather large—certainly less cramped than he had expected. The little square window—the one looking out toward the cove, doubtless—provided a brilliant, raw, but limited light, which did not reach the corners of the room, nor even its central section. Only the corner of a massive table and a few inches of rough flooring clearly emerged from the darkness. Mathias turned toward the light to look through the dirty panes.

He did not have time to recognize the landscape, for his attention was immediately drawn in the opposite direction by the noise of some utensil falling, a kitchen implement, probably. In the corner farthest from the window he could make out two silhouettes, one the fisherman's and the other, which he had not noticed up to now, that of a girl or young woman—slender, graceful, and wearing a close-fitting dress which was either black or very dark. Her head did not reach to the man's shoulder. She leaned over, bending her knees, to pick up the fallen object. Motionless above her, his hands on his hips, the sailor bent his head a little, as if to gaze at her.

Behind them were flames appearing through a circular opening in a horizontal surface—short yellow flames spreading sideways in order not to extend beyond the level of the opening. They issued from the grate of a large kitchen stove standing against the rear wall from which one of the two cast-iron lids had been removed.

Mathias walked around the big table to join the couple; but not the slightest attempt was made at an introduction, nor any other kind of speech. His exuberance gone now, the host's expression was severe, his half-closed eyes producing a line across his brow portending either anxiety or anger. Something must have happened, while the salesman

had his back turned, between him and the girl—his daughter?
—his wife?—a servant?

They sat down at the table in silence. There was nothing
on it but two soup plates, two glasses, and an ordinary
hammer. The two men sat facing the window, each at an
end of the long bench running the length of the table. The
sailor uncorked the two bottles of wine one after the other
with a corkscrew attached to his pocket knife. The woman
set another glass and plate for Mathias; then she brought a
casserole of boiled potatoes and finally, without bothering
to put them on a plate, two whole broiled spider-crabs.
Then she sat down on a stool facing the salesman—between
him and the window, her back to the light.

Mathias tried to see through the panes. The sailor poured
the wine. In front of them the two crabs were lying side
by side, the angular legs in the air, half-crooked toward
their bellies. Looking at the simple cotton dress worn by the
girl opposite him, Mathias decided he was getting too warm.
He took off his duffle coat, threw it on a box behind the
bench, and unbuttoned his jacket. He regretted having let
himself be brought all the way to this cottage, where he
felt alien, importunate, as if he inspired defiance in its
inhabitants, and where, furthermore, his presence was justified by no hope of a sale, as he might have guessed.

His two companions had begun to peel their potatoes,
using their nails with deliberate movements. The salesman
reached into the casserole and imitated them.

Suddenly the fisherman burst out laughing, so unexpectedly that Mathias gave a start; his eyes shifted from the
girl's black dress to his neighbor's suddenly cheerful face.
The man's glass was empty again. Mathias drank a swallow
from his own.

"It's damned funny all the same!" said the man.

The salesman wondered if he should answer. He decided

it was more discreet to busy himself with his task, facilitated by the unusual length of his nails. He looked at the thin, close-fitting black dress, and the reflections of the light playing about the base of the girl's neck.

"When I think," the man said, "that here we are, the two of us, calmly peeling potatoes together. . . ." He laughed and left his sentence unfinished. Indicating the crabs with his chin, he asked, "Don't you like hookers?"

Mathias answered in the affirmative, asked himself the same question, and decided that he had just lied. The odor, however, was not disagreeable. The sailor picked up one of the creatures and tore off its limbs one by one; with the largest blade of his knife he pierced the belly at two points and then stripped off the carapace with a precise, vigorous gesture; the body in one hand and the shell in the other, he stopped a moment to inspect the flesh.

"And they claim they're empty!"

This exclamation was followed by several insults intended for the fish merchants, and the man finished with a few recriminations about the low prices spider-crabs were bringing now. At the same time he had taken the hammer and begun to break open the legs with sharp taps, using the table between his own plate and the salesman's as an anvil.

As he was struggling with a particularly difficult joint, a little liquid squirted out, spattering against the girl's cheek. She said nothing but wiped it off with the back of her forefinger. She was wearing a gold circlet which might have been a wedding-ring.

The sailor continued his monologue, speaking in turn of the increasing difficulties of life for the islanders, of the development of the village at Black Rocks in recent years, of the electricity which a large part of the countryside was now installing, of his objections to the extension of the current to this house, of the "good life" he led here in his corner of the cliff, "with the little girl," among his traps and nets. The conversation presented no problems for Mathias, the other man never requiring an answer, even when he happened to speak in interrogation; on such occasions it was enough to wait until a few silent seconds had passed and then the monologue continued as if there had been no interruption.

From all appearances, the sailor preferred keeping to generalities rather than dwelling on his own experiences. Not once did he refer to the friendship which had bound Mathias and himself together for that vague period the salesman vainly attempted to determine in time. Sometimes the fisherman spoke to him as to his own brother, immediately afterward treating him as a guest or a casual visitor. The diminutive "Matt," which he employed in his bursts of intimacy, provided no illumination, for he could remember no one who had ever called him by this name.

There was no greater specification of place or circumstance than of date or duration. In Mathias' opinion, their friendship could scarcely have originated on the island—for all kinds of reasons—unless it was connected with his earliest youth. But the man was not speaking of his youth. On the contrary, he expatiated at length on the new system of lenses which had been installed in the lighthouse last autumn, attaining an unprecedented optic power capable of piercing the heaviest fog. He undertook to explain their operation, but his description of the apparatus, despite a certain technical jargon, was from the start so obscure that the salesman did not even try to follow its course. It seemed to him that his host was using the words without understanding their meaning, satisfied to set one here or there, almost at chance, into the surface of his discourse, which was itself quite vague and meaningless. He emphasized most of his sentences with rapid, expansive, complicated gestures which seemed only remotely connected with what he was saying. The various joints of one of the big claws thus described above the table a trajectory of circles, spirals, loops, and figure eights; since the shell had been broken, tiny fragments fell off and landed all around them. The crab and his own garrulity making him thirsty, the man frequently interrupted himself to refill his glass.

In the girl's glass, on the contrary, the level remained the same. She said nothing and ate scarcely at all. After each piece she swallowed, she carefully licked her fingers clean —perhaps in honor of their guest. She rounded her mouth, pushed out her lips, and passed her fingers between them several times, from back to front. To see better what she was doing, she half turned toward the window.

"It lights up the cliff like broad daylight," declared the fisherman in conclusion.

It was obviously untrue: the beam of the lighthouse did not reach the coast below them. An astonishing error on the part of a man who was supposed to be a sailor; yet he seemed to think that this was its function, doubtless in order to show navigators the detail of the rocks to be avoided. He probably never used his fishing-smack at night.

The "little girl" was sitting perfectly still, profile toward him, her middle finger in her mouth. Leaning forward, her head was bent; the outline of the nape of her neck, rounded and taut, gleamed in the light behind her.

But she was not half-turned toward the light to make sure she was cleaning her hand thoroughly. Her eyes, as far as Mathias could judge from where he was sitting, were looking sideways at the corner of the window, as if trying to make out something through the dirty pane.

"It's the whip she deserves, that trollop!"

At first the salesman did not know what his host was talking about, for he has not been paying attention to what had gone before. When he realized he was referring to the youngest Leduc girl, Mathias wondered how the sailor had managed to shift the conversation to such a subject. Nevertheless, he took advantage of a pause to agree with the master of the house: after everything he had heard since morning it really seemed that the girl deserved a good whipping, perhaps an even worse punishment.

At this moment he discovered that the sailor was looking in his direction. He glanced to his left; the man was staring at him with so profound an expression of astonishment that Mathias himself was surprised. After all, he had said nothing remarkable. Was it only because his interlocutor did not expect an answer? Mathias tried to remember if he had said anything else since he had come into the cottage. He was unable to be sure: perhaps he had said that the room was warm—perhaps some banality about the lighthouse. . . . He swallowed a mouthful of wine and sighed as he put down his glass: "Children are a lot of trouble."

But he was relieved to see that the fisherman was no longer concerned with him; his face had grown serious again, preoccupied as it had been before. He stopped talking, his hands empty, inert, his forearms leaning on the edge of the table. His gaze—over the remains of the crab, the empty bottle, the full bottle, the shoulder under the black cotton—was unquestionably toward the little window.

"Rain tomorrow," he said.

He was still not moving. After about twenty seconds he corrected himself: "Tomorrow—or the day after for sure."

In any case, the salesman would be far away.

Without changing position, the fisherman said: "If it's that Jacqueline you're watching for . . ."

Mathias supposed he was speaking to his young companion, but nothing gave him the slightest clue. She had begun to toy with her food again, and behaved as if she had not heard. The man continued: "You can hope I'll give her a fine reception."

He emphasized the word "fine" to show that it should be taken in the opposite sense. Furthermore, like most islanders, he used "hope" instead of "imagine"—which in the present case seemed more likely to mean "fear."

"She won't come now," the salesman said.

He wished he had not spoken, and merely increased his confusion by adding far too hurriedly: "I mean, she must have gone to lunch by now."

He glanced anxiously around him: luckily no one seemed to have noticed his interruption or his embarrassment. The girl had lowered her eyes over a piece of shell into which she was trying to insert the tip of her tongue. Over the outline of her shoulder which the thin cloth divided into two parts—one flesh, the other black—the man was looking toward the window.

In a low though distinct voice he pronounced these words: ". . . with the crabs . . .," which seemed to have no relation to anything at all, and then burst out laughing for the second time.

Mathias' sudden fear gave way to a sense of confusion and lassitude. He tried to find something to cling to in his distress, but found only fragments. He wondered what he was doing there. He wondered what he had done for an hour or more: in the fisherman's cottage . . . along the top of the cliff . . . in the village café . . .

In the cottage, at this moment, there was a man sitting at the table whose face (eyes half-closed) was turned toward a little window. His strong, inert, empty hands, half-open, showed his long nails which were slightly curved, like claws. In passing his eyes grazed the slender, smooth neck of the young woman who was also sitting at the table, as motionless as he, keeping her eyes lowered on her own hands.

Sitting at the man's right and facing the girl, at an equal distance from each, Mathias imagined exactly what could be seen from where his neighbor was sitting. . . . In the fisherman's cottage, at this moment, he was eating lunch, waiting until it was time for him to continue his rounds. To get here, he had had to walk along the cliff top with his host—the old friend he had met in the village. As for the café, hadn't he managed to sell one of his wrist watches there?

Nevertheless, these justifications did not manage to satisfy him. Casting back still further, he asked himself what he was doing on the road between the town and the lighthouse, then in the town itself, then earlier still . . .

What had he been doing, then, since morning? This whole extent of time seemed to him long, uncertain, unaccounted for—not so much, perhaps, because of the small number of items sold, as because of the casual and unsystematic way in which these sales had been conducted, which also applied to the sales that had not succeeded, and even the intervening expeditions.

He would have preferred to go at once. But he could hardly leave his hosts so abruptly, without even knowing if the meal was over. The complete lack of form which presided over the latter's arrangement prevented the salesman once again from knowing what to do. Here too he found himself unable to act according to any rule he could interpret as applicable—which might serve as an example for his conduct—behind which he could have entrenched himself.

The state of things around him furnished no point of reference: the meal had no more reason to be over than it had to continue. An empty bottle stood next to one that was still untouched (although uncorked); one of the crabs had been scattered about in innumerable shreds of shell, scarcely identifiable now, while the other, still intact, lay as before on its spiny back, its angular legs bent inward toward a central point on the belly where the whitish cara-pace showed a y-shaped star; about half the potatoes were still left in the casserole.

No one was eating any more, however.

The regular sound of the waves dashing against the rocks at the entrance to the cove almost imperceptibly filled the silence, remotely at first, but soon drowning the whole room in its swelling volume.

The head bent in front of the window, with the light behind it, turned to the left—exposing all four square panes to view—in profile again, but this time in the opposite direc-tion: the forehead toward the darkest corner, the nape of the neck in full light. Just above the black cloth at the nape of the neck, appeared a long, fresh scratch, the kind left by brambles on a skin that is too tender. The tiny pearls of blood along its length seemed to be still wet.

A wave broke, farther off, almost inaudibly—or else it beat, Mathias counted to nine; a wave broke. On the panes the former course of raindrops could be traced in the dust. In front of this window, one rainy day when they had left him alone in the house, he had spent all afternoon drawing a sea gull perched on one of the fence posts at the end of the garden. He had often heard the story before.

The head returned to its original position in front of the panes, above the soup plate full of spider-crab legs broken into tiny red and white fragments.

A wave broke, farther off, almost inaudibly—or else it was only the sound of breathing—the salesman's, for instance.

He recalled the movement of the water rising and falling against the verticle embankment.

Nearer, on his own plate, he found the same red and white accumulation of blades and needles. Once again the water covered the marks made by the iron ring.

He was on the point of making the gestures and speaking the words which would automatically lead to his departure —looking at his watch, saying, "It is already such and such an hour," suddenly standing up and apologizing for having to. . . , etc.—when the sailor, making a sudden decision, stretched his right hand toward the casserole, seized a potato, and brought it close to his eyes, too close, really, as if to examine it near-sightedly—but with his mind elsewhere, perhaps. Mathias thought he was going to begin peeling it. Nothing of the kind occurred. The tip of his thumb was passed slowly over the surface of a large, gnarled-looking excrescence, then after a few moments more of this silent observation, the potato rejoined the rest in the bottom of the casserole.

"The blight's starting again," the fisherman murmured to himself.

Doubtless the preceding subject of conversation was closer to his heart, for he immediately returned to it. He had, he said, run into Maria Leduc, one of the two older girls, who was out looking for her sister Jacqueline "one more time." He bestowed upon the latter a number of insulting names, of which the most emphatic ranged from "hellcat" to "little vampire"; warming to his subject, he shouted that she would never again set foot in his house, that he was even forbidding her to come near the place, and that he didn't advise "her" to try seeing her on the sly anywhere else. "Her" was the girl sitting opposite Mathias. She did not react to these threats, even when the man, standing up in anger, leaned across the table as if he were going to strike her.

His violence somewhat abated, he spoke cryptically of the Leduc girl's crimes—still the same ones—which seemed to the salesman, on this new hearing, even more obscure than they had been before. Instead of a straight-forward account of this or that act, there were only—as usual—involved allusions to matters of a psychological or moral order, lost in an interminable series of consequences and causes among which the responsibilities of the protagonists disappeared altogether.

. . . Julian, the bakery apprentice, had almost drowned himself the week before. Besides Jacqueline Leduc, several other people were involved, if not with the event, at least with the story the sailor told about it; in particular, a young fisherman called "little Louis" and his fiancee—"his ex-fiancee," to be more exact, since she now refused to marry him. Louis was just twenty, Julian was two years younger. A quarrel had broken out between them on Sunday evening. . . .

But Mathias could not determine to what degree the girl was the subject of this quarrel, nor whether it was a matter of attempted murder or attempted suicide, or merely an accident. The fiancee's role was not confined, furthermore, merely to breaking off her engagement (she had probably only threatened to break it off); as for the older friend who had repeated to the baker's apprentice his rival's words—distorting them somewhat, it seemed . . .

It seemed to Mathias that the sailor was particularly irritated with the two youths for not agreeing to drown the girl. Lest he be suspected of avoiding the discussion of Violet's misdeeds and their necessary punishment, the salesman did not dare manifest his eagerness to continue on his way. He even decided it would look better if he took an active part. His host having started on a eulogy of "that poor Leduc woman," Mathias decided to tell about his morning visit to the three girls' mother; as he did not recall a single detail concerning the approaching marriages of the two older daughters, he was constrained to improvise. Then he mentioned his friendship with their uncle Joseph, who worked for the steamship line in the city. Speaking of a recent conversation he had had with the latter on the quay, just before sailing, he proceeded quite naturally to a complete account of his day. He had got up, he said, very early in order to catch the boat, for he had to make the long trip between his house and the harbor on foot. He had walked fast, without stopping once. He had arrived a little too early to go on board, and had taken advantage of the remaining time to sell his first watch to a sailor of the line. He had been less fortunate since landing on the island —at least at first. Altogether, though, he couldn't complain about his morning—thanks of course to the pains he took to prepare his sales trips in every detail. According to his plans made the day before, he had begun with the houses along the harbor; having then rented a good bicycle, he had headed toward Black Rocks, stopping at every door, and even leaving the main road here and there to visit isolated dwellings whenever it seemed worth it. That was how he had happened to sell one of his finest models at the Marek farm. All these side-trips took a negligible amount of time, for the bicycle he had rented worked perfectly—it was a real pleasure to ride on it. The sales themselves were sometimes transacted with astonishing speed: it was enough to open his suitcase, and the quality of the merchandise immediately gained him customers. Press the clasp, open the cover, etc. . . . This had happened, for example, in the case of the couple who lived along the road just before you reached the village at the lighthouse. A little farther on, at the village café, the salesman had just sold another watch and was getting ready to have his lunch, when he met his old friend Jean Robin, and had immediately been invited here for lunch.

Mathias had then followed him to his cottage, situated just beyond the village in a little cove near the sea. They had begun dinner at once, exchanging old recollections and discussing the changes that had occurred in the countryside since those days. Afterward, the salesman had shown them his line of watches, but without delaying long, for he had to continue his rounds according to the established schedule in order to be back at the harbor before the boat left—at four-fifteen.

First he had finished the systematic canvassing of the village at Black Rocks, where he had managed to sell several more watches—including three to a single family, the one that ran the grocery–general store. He had also found the two fishermen he had met an hour before, at the café. One of them had bought a watch.

Once beyond the village, the road followed the coast east, but at a certain distance from the cliff, across a moor as barren of bushes as of houses. The ocean, because of the rolling ground, remained generally invisible. Mathias pedaled rapidly, impelled rather than impeded by the wind. The sky was quite overcast. It was neither cold nor hot.

The road, narrower and less well-kept than that leading from town to the lighthouse, was nevertheless satisfactorily paved—broad enough, in any case, for a bicycle. In this almost deserted section of the island—and off the main arteries—there was probably never much traffic. The road made a large semicircular curve which reached the farthest point of the island and then curved back toward the center. It was on this last portion, extending from the seaboard villages to the southwest section of town, that he might meet a cart or an old automobile. But on the less-frequented part, toward the tip of the island, the traffic was so rare that patches of low vegetation had invaded the sides of the road in some places, while the wind, at others, accumulated little beaches of dust and sand in which the bicycle left its tracks. Crushed into the surface of the road—no toad, no frog.

No streak of shadow could be seen lying across the road, since there was neither telegraph pole nor sunshine. Having already crossed the narrow passageway between the dried corpse and the rounded extremity of the pole, old Madame Marek would have continued on her way without seeing him.

The salesman, at the last moment, had had to call out to her in order to be recognized. After having inquired why he had found the farm deserted and locked, he turned to the object of his visit: the sale of wrist watches. There, at the roadside, he had gained his first success on the island.

He tried to calculate from memory the total amount received since he had landed. First of all there was old Madame Marek: one hundred fifty-five crowns; next, the exhausted-looking couple: one hundred fifty-five crowns, making three hundred ten; then the proprietress of the café: two hundred seventy-five—and three hundred ten: five hundred eighty five . . . five hundred eighty-five . . . five hundred eighty-five. . . . The next transaction had not been a sale but a gift: he had made a present of a gold-plated lady's watch to the girl . . . or young woman . . .

As a matter of fact there had been a third person at lunch at Jean Robin's. It was to her that Mathias had shown his collection, since the sailor was obviously uninterested. (Standing in front of the little window, he was looking outside.) The salesman had set down his suitcase at the end of the long table—pressing the clasp, folding back the cover, moving aside the memorandum book . . .—the girl, who was beginning to clear the table, had come closer to look.

He took the cardboard strips out of the suitcase one by one; she admired them without saying a word, opening her eyes very wide. He stepped back a little to let her examine his wares as long as she liked.

Over her shoulder, he saw her fingering a gold-plated watch strap, then the case itself, more slowly. Twice— once in one direction, then in the other—her middle finger followed the circular shape. She was slender and graceful, bending her neck at the nape—under his eyes—within reach of his hand.

Leaning over a little, he says: "Which do you like best?"

Still without answering, without turning around, she picks up the cardboard strips one by one. Exposed by the rounded collar of her dress, a long scratch studded with red pearls tears across the tender skin of her neck. Mathias imperceptibly stretches out his hand.

He checks the gesture at once. The arm falls back. He has not tried to stretch out his hand. Slender and graceful, the young woman bends her head a little lower, exposing the nape of her neck and the long scratch at its base. The tiny pearls of blood seem to be still wet.

"This one is the prettiest."

After the story about Violet, the fisherman had again begun on some general considerations of life on the island— oddly contradictory though they were. Each time that he seemed to want to illustrate what he was saying by some more personal detail, the latter contradicted the very point of view he was defending. In spite of this, the general tone of his remarks retained—in appearance, at least—a coherent structure, so that a distracted attention would not realize the anomalies involved.

It was to have a pretext for leaving the table—the first step toward departure—that Mathias had proposed showing the watches. He could not delay any longer, for he had to finish his rounds and return to the harbor before four-fifteen.

Suitcase, clasp, cover, black memorandum book . . .

Having glanced distractedly at the first cardboard strip, the fisherman turned his back to look out the window. His companion, on the contrary, came closer to look. It occurred to Mathias that he might thank her for her hospitality by making her a present of one of the cheaper watches, which at her age would still make her happy.

Afterward, he returned to the village, which he quickly finished canvassing. He managed to sell several more watches—including three to a single family, the one that ran the grocery–general store.

After Black Rocks, the road ran east along the coast, but at a certain distance from the cliff, and turned inland after the fork leading to the nearby point—where there was no house to interest the salesman—toward the seaboard villages extending to the southwest section of town. Mathias, who was riding very fast, hurrying because of the lateness of the hour, soon found himself among the first houses. He managed to make a good many sales without wasting too much time, as many in the little clusters of houses as in the isolated cottages that marked the intervals between them. Encouraged by his success, he even made excursions off the main road (venturing farther inland again), returning to the coast at an important fishing village—the last before the big pier, the harbor dominated by its ruined fortifications, the flat housefronts along the quay, the landing slip, and the little steamer which was doubtless already preparing for departure.

But the salesman did not take advantage of the short cut which would have brought him directly to the harbor. His watch indicated barely three o'clock, and according to his schedule he still had to explore the whole northwest section of the island—that is, the wild and sparsely settled west coast to the left of the lighthouse, then the steep peninsula called "Horses Point," symmetrical to the one he was now heading for, and finally the villages—or rather the groups of farmhouses—scattered between the point and the fort, located inland for the most part, so that he would not even try the least accessible ones if his time was running short.

For the moment he had more than an hour ahead of him, and if he hurried he could make up for his delay without difficulty. He therefore returned to the main road and kept to his prescribed course.

Almost at once he was at the point where the road to Black Rocks, which he had taken this morning after leaving town, crossed the main road. To his right the town began some five hundred yards away at the bottom of the hill, with the house where the widow Leduc lived with her three daughters. To the left would be the fork leading to the mill. Actually the salesman did not remember the landscape precisely enough to situate these elements with much assurance. He had barely noticed the crossroads in passing. But he had no doubt that it was indeed this crossroads, and that was the important thing. Besides, Mathias did not have time, on this second occasion, to worry any more about it.

As he rode along he mechanically looked at his watch again, to reassure himself that he was not too late to begin this last section of his itinerary—the big loop from the cliff to Horses Point and back. He continued straight on his way; the hands had virtually not moved at all. Since there was no traffic at the crossroads, he did not even have to slow down.

He touched his suitcase with his fingertips to be sure it was still there on the luggage rack—where he had finally fastened it in an ingenious way that permitted him to remove and replace it promptly. Then he looked down at the movement of the pedals, the chain, the gearing, the wheels that turned without any grinding noise. A film of dust was beginning to cover the chromium tubing.

Pedaling still faster, he was now traveling at a speed that astonished the few people he passed coming toward him; those he passed from behind sometimes gave an exclamation of surprise—or of fear.

He came to a sudden halt in front of the traditional clumps of mahonia and dismounted. He knocked at the window-panes, leaned his bicycle against the wall, picked up the suitcase, entered at once. . . . Hallway, first door to the right, kitchen, the big oval table covered with an oilcloth patterned with little flowers, opening the clasp, etc. . . . When the customer looked dubious, Mathias waited no more than a few moments; often he left without even having unpacked his collection. With practice, thirty seconds are enough to tell the ones that will never buy anything.

Along this coast, many farmhouses were in ruins, or in such disrepair that there was no reason to visit them.

There was a fork to the right which certainly led to town. Mathias continued straight ahead.

The road, unfortunately, became rather bad. Since he did not want to slow down, the salesman was severely jolted by the irregularities of the terrain. He tried as much as he could to avoid the most evident holes, but their number and depth constantly increased, making his progress increasingly hazardous.

The entire surface of the road was soon nothing more than holes and humps. The bicycle was shaken by a continual jarring, and at every rotation of the wheels bucked against huge stones; his precious burden was threatened with one bad fall after another. In spite of his efforts, Mathias was losing speed.

The wind off the point was not as strong as was to be feared. The edge of the cliff, higher than the adjoining moor, protected the latter somewhat. Nevertheless, the salesman, who here received it full in the face, found the wind an additional impediment.

From now on he stopped with relief here and there to show his merchandise. But luck was less with him in this part of the country. In the few homes into which he made his way, he found only undecided and quibbling people with whom it was impossible to come to an agreement.

He failed to make two sales after having wasted much more time than usual, believing at every moment that a decision would finally be reached and that only one more complimentary moment would keep him from regretting all that had already passed. When he left the second of these houses, having failed completely, he consulted his watch with a certain uneasiness. It was a little after three-thirty.

Leaping onto the seat without bothering to fasten the suitcase to the luggage rack, he began pedaling as hard as he could, holding the handlebars with one hand and the imitation-leather handle of his suitcase in the other.

Luckily the road from here on was in slightly better condition. After the first village on the north coast, it became quite good in fact. The road now led to the fort and then the town. The wind was once again behind him—or almost.

He rode on at a steady speed, although conscious of a slight nervousness.

The houses were becoming a little more numerous—and less poverty-stricken—but whether it was because the salesman presented his wares too hurriedly, or simply did not permit his customers the minimum amount of time indispensable to country people's decisions, Mathias did not make as many sales as he had anticipated.

He made the first scheduled side-trip—a very short one—at the old Roman tower near the village of Saint-Sauveur. He was cordially received but managed to sell only one watch—and from the cheapest series.

When he looked at his watch again, it was already ten minutes to four.

He calculated rapidly that at most a mile and a quarter separated him from the little triangular square where he would leave the bicycle at the café–tobacco shop–garage. Without side-trips, it would take him about ten minutes to get there, including the short walk from the tobacco shop to the boat and the thirty seconds he needed to pay the garageman.

He had just under a quarter of an hour until then. The salesman would have time enough to try his luck at a few last doors.

Rushing on as if he were being pursued, running, bounding, throwing himself about—but without wasting his strength in gesticulations—he persisted until the last possible moment. Leaving matters somewhat up to chance, as soon as a house along the road seemed to look rather prosperous, or less ramshackle, or newer, he jumped off the bicycle and raced to the door, suitcase in hand.

Once. . . . Twice. . . . Three times . . .

When he found a window open on the ground floor, he spoke from outside, ready to show his merchandise from where he stood. Otherwise he walked into the kitchen without even knocking. Sometimes he economized on words and gestures—excessively, even.

As a matter of fact, all of these attempts were useless. He was going too fast: he was taken for a madman.

At five after four he caught sight of the fort. Now he would have to get back to town without stopping again. There were only three hundred yards or so to travel uphill, then the slope down to the harbor. He wanted to go faster still.

The bicycle chain began to make an unpleasant sound—

as if it were rubbing sidways against the sprocket-wheel. Mathias pedaled vigorously.

But the grinding noise grew more pronounced so rapidly that he decided to get off and examine the transmission. He set his suitcase down on the ground and crouched over the machine.

There was no time to study the phenomenon in detail. He confined himself to pushing the sprocket-wheel back toward the frame—dirtying his fingers as little as possible—and started off again. The abnormal friction seemed to grow worse.

He got off again at once and twisted the axle of the sprocket-wheel in the opposite direction.

As soon as he was back on the seat again he realized that matters were going from bad to worse. He was making no progress at all: the machinery was almost completely jammed. Trying another remedy, he manipulated the gear-shift—once, twice, three times—pedaling at the same time. As soon as it reached its maximum gear expansion, the chain sprang away from the sprocket-wheel.

He got off the bicycle, set down the suitcase, and lay the machine on its side in the road. It was eight minutes after four. This time, while adjusting the chain in place on the little toothed wheel, he covered himself with grease. He was sweating.

Without wiping his hands he seized his suitcase, mounted the bicycle again, and tried to pedal. The chain sprang away from the sprocket-wheel.

He put it back a second time, then a third. He tried it on all three gear-wheels, without managing to make it hold on any: it came off at the first revolution. Giving up, he continued on foot, half-running, half-walking, holding the suitcase in his left hand and with his right pushing the bicycle.

An essential piece of the machinery must have been broken during the jolting on the bad road from Horses Point.

Mathias had just begun walking down the slope to town when he suddenly realized he might be able to coast down without using the pedals. He got back on the bicycle and impelled himself forward with a vigorous kick. For balance he pressed the hand carrying the suitcase against the left grip of the handlebars.

Now he had to be careful not to disturb the chain which he had put back around the sprocket-wheel—therefore he must not move his feet, or he would make it spring off again and tangle with the rear-wheel spokes. In order to fasten the chain more firmly to the sprocket-wheel, since it no longer had to revolve, the salesman thought of attaching it with a piece of cord he had picked up that morning; he began looking for the cord in the pockets of his duffle coat. But not finding it in either one, he remembered. . . . He remembered that he no longer had it.

Furthermore, he had arrived without mishap at the level section of the road just before the fork; he was forced to stop in order to avoid a little girl who was heedlessly crossing just in front of him. In order to gain momentum he unthinkingly gave the pedals a turn . . . then several more. The bicycle was working perfectly. The peculiar noise had entirely disappeared.

At the other end of the town he heard the little steamer's whistle: once, twice, three times.

He entered the square, the town hall on his left. The whistle blew again, shrill and prolonged.

On the movie bulletin-board, the advertisement had been changed. He leaned the bicycle against it and dashed into the café–tobacco shop. No one was there: no customer in the room, no proprietor behind the counter. He called. No one answered.

Outside there was no one either, no one in sight. Mathias remembered that the man had returned his security. The sum amounted to . . .

The ship's whistle blew a long blast—in a slightly lower tone.

The salesman jumped onto the bicycle. He would leave it at the end of the quay—would hand it to someone—with the amount he owed for its rental. But even pedaling as hard as he could along the uneven cobbles, he managed to remember that the garageman had still not told him the terms. At first it had only been a question of the two-hundred-crowns security, which obviously bore no relation to the value of the bicycle nor to the cost of a half-day's rental.

Mathias decided not to try riding along the pier, for it was encumbered with a great many baskets and hampers. There was not a single stroller on this part of the quay to take the money, so he abandoned the bicycle against the parapet and immediately ran toward the steamer. In a few seconds he had reached the landing slip, where a little crowd of about ten people was standing. The gangplank had been pulled up. The steamer was slowly pulling away from the embankment.

The tide was high now. The water covered a good part of the inclined plane—half of it, perhaps—or two-thirds. The seaweed on the bottom could no longer be seen, nor the tufts of greenish moss which made the lower stones so slippery.

Mathias looked at the narrow strip of water almost imperceptibly widening between the ship's side and the oblique edge of the landing slip. He could not jump across it, not so much because of the distance—which was still very slight—but because of the dangers of landing on the gunwale or in the midst of the passengers and their baggage on the stern deck. The downward slope along which he would have to run to gain momentum increased the difficulty still further, as did the heavy shoes and the duffle coat he was wearing, not to mention the suitcase he was carrying.

He looked at the half-turned backs of the people staying behind, their faces in profile, their stares motionless and parallel—meeting identical stares from the ship. Standing against an iron pillar that supported the deck above, a child of seven or eight was gravely staring at him with large, calm eyes. He wondered why she was looking at him that way, but then something—a silhouette—came between him and the image—a sailor on board whom the salesman thought he recognized. He ran forward three steps toward the end of the pier and shouted: "Hey there!"

The sailor did not hear him over the noise of the engines. On the pier Mathias' immediate neighbors turned toward him—then others farther away, by degrees.

The passengers, noticing the general movement of heads on the pier, also looked in his direction—as if in astonishment. The sailor raised his eyes and caught sight of Mathias, who waved his arms in his direction and cried again: "Hey there!"

"Hey!" answered the sailor waving his arms in farewell. The little girl next to him had not moved, but the maneuver executed by the ship changed the direction of her gaze: now she would be looking at the top of the pier, above the landing slip, where another group of people was standing on the narrow passageway that led to the beacon light. These too were now facing Mathias. All of them had the same strained, frozen expression as before.

Without addressing anyone in particular, Mathias said: "I didn't miss it by much."

The little steamer executed its usual maneuver, which

consisted of turning so that it presented its stem to the open sea. The islanders left the end of the pier one after the other to return to their houses. The salesman wondered where he would sleep that night, and the next, and the one after that too—for the boat would not return until Friday. He also wondered if there were any policemen on the island. Then he decided it wouldn't change matters, whether there were or not.

In any case, it would have been better if he had left, since that had been his plan.

"You should have shouted! They would have come back."

Mathias turned toward the person who had spoken these words. It was an old man in city clothes whose smile might have been kindly as well as ironic.

"Bah!" answered Mathias. "It doesn't matter."

Besides, he *had* shouted—not right away, it was true—and not very insistently. The sailor had not seemed to understand that he had just missed the boat. He did not know why he had shouted himself.

"They would have come back," the old man repeated. "At high tide they can turn easily."

Perhaps he wasn't joking. "I didn't have to go," said the salesman.

Besides, he had to take back the bicycle and pay for its rental. He looked at the water lapping against the foot of the embankment—slack tide probably. In the sheltered angle of the landing slip, the backwash produced scarcely any swell at all.

Then came a series of little waves from the steamer's propeller. But the harbor was empty. Only a fishing-smack was dancing out in the middle somewhere, its mast waving to and fro. Since he risked getting spattered on the landing slip, Mathias walked up the slope and found himself again on top of the pier, walking alone among the baskets, nets, and traps.

He put his right hand—the free one—in the pocket of his duffle coat. It came into contact with the slender cord rolled into a figure eight—a fine piece for his collection. He had often heard the story before: once he had had a whole boxful—perhaps twenty-five or thirty years ago.

He did not remember what had become of them. The slender cord picked up that morning had also disappeared from his duffle coat pocket. His right hand encountered only a pack of cigarettes and a little bag of gumdrops.

Thinking this was a good time to have a smoke, he took out the pack and discovered that several cigarettes were already missing—three, to be exact. He put the pack back in his pocket. The bag of gumdrops had also been opened.

He was walking slowly along the pier, on the side with no railing. The water level was several yards higher. At the end of the pier, against the quay, the sea had entirely covered the strip of mud. Beyond stretched the row of houses and shops: the hardware store at the corner of the square, the butcher shop, the café "A l'Espérance," the shop that sold everything—women's lingerie, wrist watches, fish, preserves, etc. . . .

Groping at the bottom of his pocket, Mathias opened the cellophane bag and took out a gumdrop. This one was wrapped in blue paper. Still using only one hand, he unwrapped the paper, put the gumdrop in his mouth, rolled the little rectangle of paper into a ball, and threw it into the water where it floated on the surface.

Leaning over a little farther, he saw at his feet the vertical embankment that plunged into the black water. The strip of shadow cast by the pier would have grown very thin at this time of day. But there was no longer any sunshine; the sky was uniformly overcast.

Mathias advanced to the middle of the cluster of gray parallel lines between the water level and the outer edge of the parapet: the inner rim of the parapet, the angle formed by the jetty and the base of the parapet, the side of the pier that had no railing—rigid horizontal lines, interrupted by several openings, extending straight toward the quay.

III

The new advertisement represented a landscape.

At least Mathias thought he could make out a moor dotted with clumps of bushes in its interlacing lines, but something else must have been superimposed: here and there certain outlines or patches of color appeared which did not seem to be part of the original design. On the other hand they could not be said to constitute another drawing entirely; they appeared to have no relation to one another, and it was impossible to guess their intention. They succeeded, in any case, in so blurring the configurations of the moor that it was doubtful whether the poster represented a landscape at all.

On the upper section appeared the names of the leading actors—foreign names Mathias thought he had already seen many times, but which he associated with no particular faces. Underneath was spread in huge letters what must have been the name of the film: "Monsieur X on the Double Circuit." Not conforming to the trends of recent productions, this title—which was scarcely enticing, having little or no relation to anything human—provided remarkably little information about what type of film it described. Perhaps it was a detective story, or a thriller.

143

Attempting once again to decipher the network of curves and angles, Mathias now recognized nothing at all—it was impossible to decide whether there were two different images superimposed, or just one, or three, or even more.

He stepped back to get a better look at the bulletin-board as a whole, but the more he examined it the more vague, shifting, and incomprehensible it seemed. There were performances on Saturday night and Sunday, not before; he would be unable to see the film, since he intended to leave Friday afternoon.

"Good-looking sign, isn't it?" said a voice he knew.

Mathias raised his eyes. Above the bulletin-board the garageman's head had appeared in the doorway.

"That one, yes! . . ." the salesman began, cautiously.

"Wonder where they get colors like those," the other continued.

Did this mean that he had discovered what the lines were supposed to represent?

"Here's your bicycle," said Mathias. "It's just played me a nasty trick!"

"I'm not surprised," the garageman returned, still smiling. "All these new makes are the same—they're shiny enough, but no good when you need them."

The salesman recounted his misfortune: he had just missed the boat by a few seconds because of this chain, which at the last minute had made him lose five precious minutes.

The garageman found the incident so commonplace he did not even listen to him. He asked instead: "You came from the pier?"

"Just now . . ."

"Then you were going to take the bicycle with you?" the man exclaimed as jovially as before.

Mathias explained that he had stopped by the tobacco shop beforehand to leave the bicycle and pay for its use;

but he had found no one there. As he returned to the square—not knowing what to do next—he had heard the boat's last whistle, the one that meant the gangway was about to be closed, so he had headed toward the pier—not hurrying, since it was too late—just to watch the little steamer pull out—to have something to do, really . . .

"Yes," the man said, "I saw you. I was there too, at the end of the pier."

"Now I'm going to need a room until Friday. Where can I find one?"

The garageman seemed to be thinking it over.

"The boat left at least five minutes late today," he said, after a rather long silence.

Of course there was no hotel on the island, not even a rooming house. From time to time people rented an empty room, but it was difficult living in someone else's house, and there were really no conveniences. The best solution, as far as finding out what was available at the moment, was to ask at the café "A l'Espérance," on the quay. Then the salesman asked how much he owed for the bicycle and paid the twenty crowns he was charged. In consideration of the bicycle's newness, on the one hand, and its irregular operation on the other, it was difficult to say whether this was cheap or expensive.

"Wait a minute," the tobacconist continued, "there's the Widow Leduc just nearby—she used to have a good room to rent out; but she's off her head today, ever since her kid disappeared. You'd better leave her alone."

"Disappeared?" the salesman asked. "Madame Leduc is an old friend; I saw her only this morning. I hope nothing has happened . . ."

"It's that little Jacqueline again: they've been looking for her since noon, but no one can find her."

"She can't be far, after all! The island isn't so big as that!"

The meadows and the moor, the potato fields, the edge of the fields, the hollows in the cliff, the sand, the rocks, the sea . . .

"Don't fool yourself," said the man, winking at him. "Someone knows where she is."

Mathias did not dare leave. He had waited too long again. And now he was obliged to struggle a second time with silences that threatened to riddle the conversation at every turn: "Then that was it," he said, "that business with the sheep they were talking about at Black Rocks?"

"Yes, that's it—she was tending the sheep, but the wolf got the shepherdess!" etc. . . . etc. . . .

And also: "At thirteen! It's really a shame"—"She's got a devil inside her"—"A wild animal!"—"Children are a lot of trouble"—"She deserves to be. . . ."

There was no reason for it to stop. Mathias said something, the man answered, Mathias answered that. The man said something, Mathias answered. Mathias said something, Mathias answered. Little Jacqueline was walking along the path on top of the cliff, showing off her delicate, scandalous silhouette. In the hollows, sheltered from the wind, in the long meadow grass, under the hedges, against the trunk of a pine, she stopped and slowly ran her fingertips over her hair, her neck, her shoulders . . .

She always came home to sleep—the last house as you left town on the road to the big lighthouse. Tonight, when Mathias would climb upstairs to his room, having said good-night to the mother and the two older sisters, holding his lighted candle in front of him in his right hand and in his left his little suitcase in which he had carefully stored the cord, raising his head—he would see, a few steps higher, showing him the way up the dark staircase, so slender in her little black peasant girl's dress, Violet as a child. . . . Violet! Violet! Violet!

He pushed open the door of the café. Three sailors—one almost a boy and two older men—were sitting at a table drinking red wine. Behind the counter the girl with the timorous expression of a dog that had been whipped was leaning against the doorway of the room back of the bar, her wrists behind the small of her back. Mathias passed his hand in front of his eyes.

He asked for a room. Without a word she preceded him step by step up the narrow spiral of the suddenly darkened second staircase, gracefully slipping between the boxes and various utensils that blocked their passage. They reached the landing, the little vestibule, the room with the black and white tiling. . . . The bed had been made. The bed lamp on the night table was turned on, lighting more brightly the red material at the head of the bed, as well as several tiles, and the lambskin. On the dressing table among the jars and bottles, was the slightly tilted chromium-plated frame holding the photograph. Directly above it, the big oval mirror again reflected. . . . Mathias passed his hand in front of his eyes.

The girl had finally understood that he wanted a room as near the harbor as possible for three days. The lodging she suggested, and which he went to see at once, was not in the town proper, but just beyond, a house on the moor near the sea, just beyond the pier. This spot, despite its relative isolation, was nearer the pier than certain sections of the town itself—those, for instance, between the old harbor and the ruins of the fort.

Although of better appearance—cleaner certainly, and more frequently repainted and whitewashed than most the salesman had approached hitherto—the building, obviously the same age as the rest, presented identical physical features, the same simplified architecture: a ground floor with neither upper story nor dormers, and two identical facades,

each with two small, almost square windows on either side
of a low door. Facing the road—a secondary one which must
have been the short cut to the village Mathias had visited
before reaching Horses Point—the entrance was embellished
with the same holly-leaf mahonias, here perhaps somewhat
more flourishing.

Between the doors extended a rectilinear hallway onto
which opened all four rooms. Mathias' was the back one on
the left, overlooking the cliff.

The cliff was not very high at this point—lower, in any
case, than along the southwest beach or at the two promon-
tories at either end of the island. On the right it fell away
toward an indentation in the coast where the sea could be
seen, perhaps a third of a mile away.

From the ridge where the face of the cliff began—opposite
the house—to the house itself was a distance of no more
than three hundred yards of gently rolling moors and a
small garden that had been left fallow, although enclosed
by barbed-wire attached to wooden fence posts. The whole
landscape—low sky, patch of ocean, cliff, garden—was com-
posed of various flat, lusterless, grayish hues.

The window that looked out on it was a yard wide and
slightly higher—four panes of the same size with neither
curtains nor shade; since it was deeply recessed in the thickness of the wall, the rather large room for which it was the
only source of daylight remained virtually in darkness. Only
the heavy little table wedged into the recess received enough
light for him to write there—add up his accounts there—or
draw there.

The rest of the room was in semidarkness. Its appointments further accentuated this defect: a dull-colored carpet
and high, heavy pieces of dark furniture. The latter were
crowded so close together along all four walls that there was
some doubt whether this room was actually intended to be

lived in or merely used as a storeroom for all the discarded furniture from the rest of the house. Especially noticeable were three immense cupboards, two side by side opposite the door to the hallway. They filled almost the whole of the rear wall, leaving just enough room for a modest dressing table—this last in the dimmest corner, to the left of the window from which it was separated by two straight chairs standing against the flowered wallpaper. On the other side of the window recess, two other chairs occupied a symmetrical position. But only three of the four chairs were of the same design.

Hence, starting at the window and proceeding left (that is, counter-clockwise), were a chair, another chair, the dressing table (in the corner), a third chair, a cherrywood bed (placed lengthwise against the wall), a tiny pedestal table with a fourth chair in front of it, a commode (in the third corner), the door to the hallway, a kind of drop-leaf table that could be used as a desk when the sides were extended, and finally the third cupboard, standing diagonally across the fourth corner with the fifth and sixth chairs next to it. It was in this last, most imposing, cupboard—which was always locked—that the shoebox which harbored his string collection was kept, on the right-hand side of the lowest shelf.

The girl's body was discovered the following morning at low tide. Some fishermen—looking for the soft-shelled turtle crabs called "sleepers"—happened to find the body on the rocks under the crossroads.

The salesman heard the news while he was drinking an apéritif at the bar of the café "A l'Espérance." The sailor who was telling the story seemed quite well informed as to the location, the posture, and the state of the body; but he was not one of the men who had found it, and he did not even say if he had seen it for himself. Furthermore, he seemed completely unmoved by what he was describing. It might as well have been a stuffed doll thrown over the cliff. The man was speaking slowly and with a certain concern for accuracy, furnishing—although sometimes in scarcely logical order—all the necessary material details and offering for each some plausible explanation. Everything was clear, obvious, banal.

Little Jacqueline was lying naked on a bed of brown seaweed among the big, round rocks. Doubtless the movement of the waves had undressed her, for it was unlikely that she had been drowned while swimming—in this weather, and at such a dangerous spot. She must have lost her balance playing at the edge of the cliff, which was very steep at this point. Perhaps she had even tried to reach the water by a more or less passable rock spur which ran down on the left. She must have missed her footing, or slipped, or tried to balance on too weak a point in the rock. She had been killed by the fall—of several yards—her slender neck broken.

The hypothesis that a sudden wave might have swept her off her feet during the rising tide was no more tenable than the supposition that she had drowned while swimming: there was very little water in her lungs—much less, certainly, than if she had drowned. Besides, there were wounds on her head and limbs which corresponded more closely to a ricocheting fall against stone outcroppings than to injuries sustained by a lifeless body tossed about by the sea. Nevertheless—as might be expected—on what remained of her flesh there were also a number of bruises which resembled the result of this kind of contact.

In any case, it was difficult for nonspecialists, even those accustomed to such accidents, to establish with any certitude the origin of the different wounds and abrasions found on the girl's body; especially since the crabs, or the fish perhaps, had already begun their ravages at certain particularly tender spots. The fisherman thought that the body of an adult would have held out longer against them.

He doubted that a doctor would have anything else to say about the case, which in his opinion was unequivocal. By the same token the salesman learned that there was no doctor on the island and that the man who spoke in such a knowing way had served in the navy as a hospital attendant. There was only an old Civil Guard who as a rule confined himself to making out a death certificate.

The body had been brought to Madame Leduc's house, along with two or three pieces of the girl's clothing that had been scattered on the nearby rocks, among the seaweed. According to his informant, Madame Leduc had actually grown "rather calm" on learning what had become of her youngest daughter and the reason that had kept her from coming home. No one who witnessed the scene was surprised.

His audience—five other sailors, the proprietor, and the young barmaid—had listened to the entire account without once interrupting, merely nodding at the most decisive passages. Mathias contented himself with imitating them.

There was a pause at the end. Then the hospital attendant repeated elements of his story from first one part, then another, employing the same terms and constructing his sentences in the identical manner: "The hookers had already begun to nibble at the tenderest parts: the lips, the neck, the hands . . . other places too. . . . Only just begun, though: almost nothing. Or else it might have been a red eel, or a barbel . . ."

At last, after another silence, someone said: "It's the devil that finally punished her!"

It was one of the sailors—a young one. Several murmurs rose around him—vague sounds, signifying neither acquiescence nor protest. Then everyone was still. On the other side of the glass door, beyond the cobbles and the mud, the water of the harbor was gray, flat, and lusterless. The sun had not reappeared.

Someone spoke up behind Mathias: "Maybe she was pushed—did you ever think of that—to make her fall. . . . She was fast on her feet, that girl."

This time the silence was longer still. The salesman turned around to face the room and searched every face to discover who had just spoken.

"Anyone can lose his balance," the hospital attendant said.

Mathias emptied his glass and set it down again on the counter.

He looked at his right hand on the edge of the counter, next to the empty glass, and immediately concealed it in his duffle coat pocket. There it came in contact with the open pack of cigarettes. He took one out of the pack, still in his pocket, then put it in his mouth and lit it.

The smoke, expelled through his rounded lips, formed a great circle above the bar, slowly twisting in the calm air into two equal loops. As soon as possible Mathias would ask his landlady for a pair of scissors to cut these embarrassing nails; he did not want them to be this long for two days more. It was at that moment that he first remembered the three cigarette butts left on the cliff, in the grass, under the crossroads.

There was no harm in taking a little walk; after all, he had nothing else to do. The trip there and back would take an hour, an hour and a half at the most—he would easily be back for lunch—the visit to his old friends the Mareks—he had not found them at home the day before.

Once again he was at the bottom of the little depression, in the hollow sheltered from the wind. At least he thought he recognized it; but his recollection of it differed slightly from what was now before his eyes. The fact that the sheep were no longer there was not enough to account for the change. He tried to imagine the bicycle lying on the weeds, gleaming on the sunny slope. But the sun was missing too.

Moreover he could not find the slightest trace of a cigarette. Since all three had been only half-smoked, some passer-by might have picked them up last night or this morning. A passer-by! Nobody *passed by* in a place as remote as this—unless it happened to be the people looking for the lost shepherdess.

He glanced once more at the grass underfoot, but he no longer considered such matters important: on the island as elsewhere, everyone smoked the same brand of cigarettes —the ones in the blue pack. Nevertheless, Mathias kept his eyes on the ground. He saw the little shepherdess lying at his feet, feebly twisting from side to side. He had wadded up her shift and stuffed it into her mouth to keep her from screaming.

When he looked up again, he realized he was not alone. That was why he had looked up. Standing on the ridge fifteen or twenty yards away, a delicate silhouette was etched against the gray sky: someone was standing there, motionless, watching him.

For an instant Mathias imagined he was seeing little Jacqueline all over again. And just as he realized the absurdity of such an apparition, he noticed that the newcomer was several inches taller and several years older than she. Scrutinized carefully, moreover, this face bore no resemblance to Violet's, although it too was not unfamiliar to him. Soon he remembered: it was the young woman who lived at Jean Robin's, in the cottage at the mouth of the cove.

He walked toward her—deliberately—almost without moving. Her dress—like that of almost all the island girls—was merely a simplification of the ancient regional costume: thin, long-sleeved, and black, rather close-fitting from shoulders to hips, with a wide skirt; the rounded collar exposed the neck; the girl's hair was arranged in two short braids, one on each side of a part beginning at the nape of her neck; the braids were coiled into little buns concealing the upper part of her ears. The little girls wore practically the same dress, but much shorter and usually without sleeves; they wore their hair in the same way too, but without coiling the braids into buns.

When they went out-of-doors, the island women left their narrow, bright-colored aprons at home and wrapped big fringed shawls around their shoulders. Yet this girl wore neither apron nor shawl, nor any other outer clothing, although Mathias was wearing a duffle coat without discomfort in such weather. On the windblown ridge toward which he was walking she had to hold the folds of her skirt in one hand to keep it from rising. She half turned her head away from him, as if surprised in some misconduct.

"Hello," said Mathias. ". . . Taking a walk?"

"No," she said. And then, after a few seconds, "It's all over."

He had not noticed, yesterday, how deep her voice was. In fact he did not recall having heard her speak a word. She was rather short—as soon as their respective positions did not force him to look up at her from below, she barely reached to the salesman's shoulder.

"It's not so nice out this morning," he said.

She suddenly lifted her head, stepping back at the same time. Her eyes were red, as if she had been crying for some time. She cried out, her voice surprisingly low: "What are you looking for around here? You know perfectly well he killed her!"

And she turned her face away again, bending her neck. The fine scratch, half-scabbed over, must have opened again; the edge of her dress, as it moved, smeared a little blood over the surface of her skin.

" 'He?' Who?" asked Mathias.

"Pierre."

"Which Pierre?"

"Pierre, your friend!" she said impatiently.

Then Jean was not his name? Nor Robin either, perhaps? It was not his name written on the door panel.

She straightened up and said more calmly: "Still, it's a good thing I met you." She raised the hem of her left sleeve and removed the wrist watch beneath it—the present Mathias had given her. "I had to return this."

"You don't want it any more?"

"I have to give it back to you."

"Well, if you have to."

"He'll kill me . . . the way he killed Jackie. . ."

"Why did he kill her?"

The girl shrugged her shoulders.

"He'll kill you if you keep the watch?" Mathias asked. She turned her eyes away again: "He said you told me. . . . He said he had heard you."

"Heard what?"

"What you told me."

"And what did I tell you?"

"I don't know."

Mathias took the watch she held out to him and put it in his pocket. "Why did he kill her?" he asked.

"I don't know. . . . Jackie made fun of him."

"That's no reason."

The girl shrugged her shoulders.

"He didn't kill her," Mathias continued. "No one killed her. She fell all by herself. She slipped when she was too near the edge."

"Jackie didn't slip," the girl said.

"Look at this place—here. The ground caves in every minute. All you have to do is come a little too close. . . ."

He pointed to the edge of the cliff quite near by, but she did not even turn her eyes in that direction.

"You want to cover up," she said. "Don't worry, I won't say anything either."

"What proof would you have?"

"You heard what he was yelling yesterday, at dinner: that she wouldn't come any more now! . . . What did that mean? . . . He pushed her to get revenge. You know perfectly well he did. He was prowling around here when it happened."

Mathias thought for a few moments before answering: "You don't know what time it happened."

"But Maria was looking for her after twelve-thirty. . ."

"There was the whole morning before that."

The girl hesitated, then lowered her voice and said, almost in a whisper: "Jackie was still here after eleven."

Mathias recalled the succession of his own movements; what she was saying was quite exact. He found it irritating that this detail should be known. He asked: "How do you know?"

But her answer told him nothing he had not already guessed: the girl had paid a secret visit to her young friend out here on the cliff. She had not left her before eleven-thirty. The accident could therefore be situated within about thirty minutes of its occurrence. If his customers had noted the salesman's course with the same accuracy . . .

"Even so," he said, "that leaves a whole hour in between. . . . Plenty of time to lose your balance."

"And that was just when he was prowling around the cliff, running after me, the way he does whenever I set foot outside the house!"

"Yes . . . certainly . . . it *is* strange, all right. Tell me again what he said at dinner. 'She won't come back any more. . .'"

"'. . . now.' 'She won't come back any more now!'"

"Yes, that's it—I heard it too!"

"Then you see!"

"Perhaps you're right after all," said Mathias.

They stood without moving, neither of them speaking. Then he thought she was going to leave; but after taking two steps, she came back toward him, holding something she had been concealing in the palm of her hand.

"And then I found this, too."

It was one of the cigarettes. She pointed toward the bottom of the hollow: "I found it here, just now. People don't usually throw away half-smoked cigarettes. He had it in his mouth, the way he does in the morning, and he dropped it because Jackie was struggling."

Mathias held out his hand and took the object—to look at it more closely, supposedly. With a sudden gesture he made it disappear into his duffle coat pocket. The girl watched him with astonished eyes, her hand still stretched out to take it back. But he merely declared: "This is the actual proof that you are right."

"I wasn't going to say anything, you didn't need to take it away from me. . . . I wanted to throw it into the water. . ."

She stepped back.

Mathias forgot to answer. He saw her retreating, still staring at him, her eyes wide. Then suddenly she turned around and began to run toward the lighthouse.

When she had disappeared behind a hillock, he returned down the path by which he had come. The first thing that caught his attention—in the grass, at the bottom of the hollow sheltered from the wind—was a second half-smoked cigarette exactly like the first. He had not noticed it just now, when he had come. A tuft of grass slightly longer than the rest concealed it from view except at the very point where he happened to be standing.

Having picked it up and put it in his pocket, he began looking for the third as well, thoroughly examining the few square yards of ground where it might have fallen. But his only approximate recollection of such places prevented him from establishing the area's perimeter with much certitude.

Despite his efforts, he could not manage to discover the third cigarette. He decided it must be smaller than the other two; hence it would be less compromising—especially by itself—since it was virtually the size of the cigarette butts any smoker might throw away. No one could reasonably imagine what it had been used for.

Mathias concluded that even if this third cigarette was as little smoked as the preceding two, it could still pass for the one Jean Robin—or rather the man whose name was not Jean Robin—might have lost while he was dragging the little shepherdess toward the edge of the cliff by force. The main thing, after all, was that an eventual investigator would be unable to find more than one; for if nobody knew what they had been used for, it would be ridiculous to suspect the salesman—perhaps the only person on the whole island who had never harbored any resentment toward the girl.

On the other hand, the presence of several half-smoked cigarettes would certainly seem strange—might even suggest motives other than the vengeance of a rejected lover, if it was ever discovered, at the same time, that the wounds on the body were more suspect than those left by a fall against the rocks, the action of the sea, the ravages of fish or crabs.

Mathias would have only to destroy the two butts in his possession and claim to have thrown away the one the girl had just given him.

To gain time—all these ideas and investigations had delayed him considerably—Mathias decided to take a path back to town that would avoid the lighthouse crossroads. There were plenty to choose from among the complicated network crossing the moor. But the rolling ground prevented him from calculating his steps according to the goal to be reached—invisible from where he was—so that he had to orient himself by guesswork, deciding on an angle of approximately thirty degrees with his original direction.

He decided to follow a path that was well marked. Aside from the inconvenience of cross-country walking, it was quite likely that if he kept to such a path he might find the very short cut Maria Leduc had taken to the cliff.

Unfortunately none of the numerous existing paths coincided with the theoretical direction Mathias had selected; he was therefore confined, from the start, to one of two possible detours. Besides, every path looked winding and discontinuous—separating, reuniting, constantly interlacing, even stopping short in a briar patch. All of which obliged him to make many false starts, hesitations, retreats, posed new problems at every step, forbade any assurance as to the general direction of the path he had chosen.

Furthermore, Mathias often chose without giving much thought to the possible alternatives. Since he was walking fast, he did not have much time to think in any case. Something more serious was bothering him, something about his reasoning in the case of those three cigarettes: the one still on the cliff was not the one the young woman had picked up. Yet she was relying on its abnormal length to prove the crime. If a butt less than an inch long should now come to light, how could the salesman manage—in the eventuality of a confrontation—to make her admit it was the one she had given him? To explain the fact that it had grown shorter, it would be necessary for Mathias to have lighted it again and smoked it himself before throwing it away—an alibi which lacked both simplicity and likelihood.

His deductions and hypotheses were interrupted by his surprise at suddenly finding himself on the main road again, just opposite the road to the Marek farm—that is, not far from the milestone.

He turned around and realized that the path he was on was the very one he had taken less than an hour before, and on his bicycle yesterday afternoon. After several detours and devious curves, the junction had occurred without his noticing it.

He was not a little troubled by this discovery: at present he doubted the existence of a short cut from the town to the hollow in the cliff, whereas all his previous reflections had posited the inevitability of it. Of course the mistake delayed him still longer: he turned up for lunch almost forty minutes later that he had expected to.

This kind of inexactitude irritated as well as disturbed him, since the café had only agreed to serve him his meals as a particular favor, in the absence of any regular restaurant at this time of year. When he walked in, the proprietor pointed this out to him politely, but firmly. Mathias, breathless from running, was put out of countenance.

"I went over to see my old friends the Mareks," he gave as an excuse. "You know, near Black Rocks. They kept me longer than I expected . . ."

He immediately realized the imprudence of his words, and fell silent without adding—as he had at first intended— that Robert Marek had asked him to stay for lunch and that he had refused because he was expected here. Perhaps Robert Marek himself was leaving the café "A l'Espérance" at this very moment; it would be better not to get in any deeper. This one lie had already exposed him far too dangerously to a formal denial that risked awakening all kinds of suspicion . . .

"You came by the road from the big lighthouse, didn't you?" asked the proprietor, who had been waiting for his guest in the doorway.

"Yes, of course."

"Since you were walking, you could have taken a much shorter way. Why didn't anyone show you?"

"Probably they were afraid I might lose my way."

"It's simple enough, you just take the path behind the fields all the way. It begins here, out back." (Vague gesture of the right arm.)

It was essential for Mathias to change the subject in order to avoid any further questions about such places, or the people he had met at the farm. Fortunately the proprietor, more talkative today, shifted the conversation of his own accord to the obvious subject: the accident which had cost the youngest Leduc girl her life. Dangers of the cliff, brittleness of the rock, treachery of the ocean, disobedience of children, always doing what they're not supposed to do . . .

"To tell you the truth, it's nobody's loss, I'm sorry to say. She was a real devil! A wild animal!"

Mathias listened to this peroration with only half an ear. The business no longer interested him. The false step he had made so lightly only a moment ago preoccupied him too much: he was in constant terror his interlocutor would make some new allusion to it. A single idea possessed him: to gulp down his lunch as soon as possible and actually visit that damned farm—finally—in order to transform his lie into a mere anticipation of the truth.

Nevertheless, once out on the quay again—calmer now, feeling himself out of danger—he did not start looking for the short cut across the fields mentioned by the proprietor as well as by old Madame Marek. He turned left and headed, as usual, toward the little triangular square. He was beginning to mistrust short cuts.

He preferred the large flat stones along the quay to the uneven cobbles: it was easier to walk there. But he did not waste time staring at the exposed strip of mud—two or three yards below—which the rising tide had not yet covered. He also renounced the next temptation without difficulty:—the hardware shopwindow. In the middle of the square the monument to the dead seemed more familiar under this cloudy sky. The high circular fence with its vertical rails cast no shadow on the surrounding sidewalk. The statue on its rock pedestal was still looking toward the open sea, but no anxiety showed on its granite face. The salesman was merely going to visit some old acquaintance from whom, moreover, he would have nothing particularly startling to hear—neither good nor bad—in the way of gossip, since the old woman had already told him all their important news. His eyes happened to fall on the gaudy advertisement on the bulletin-board. He turned his head away. He was merely going to pay a visit . . . etc.

The streets were empty, which was not surprising: everyone on the island was eating dinner; it was served much later here than on the mainland; the proprietor had waited on Mathias a little ahead of time so that he himself could eat at his usual hour. The last house as you left town had its door and windows closed, like the others. The silence was reassuring, reassuring, reassuring . . .

Having climbed up the ridge, Mathias soon arrived at the junction of the two main roads—the one he was on, heading toward Black Rocks, and the one describing a kind of S from one end of the island to the other, giving access to the east and west shores—the one he had taken the day before, at the end of his rounds, to Horses Point.

A few steps farther a smaller road appeared on his right, between two retaining walls covered with gorse—a grassy path marked by a central furrow and two lateral ruts—just wide enough for a cart. Mathias decided he could scarcely appear at the farm until after dinnertime. He had plenty of time to try this path, to see if it wasn't the same one Maria Leduc had taken—the one he had not found this morning when he left the cliff.

Unlike the paths across the moor, this one gave him no chance to choose the wrong fork: it ran along between low embankments or fieldstone walls: regular, continuous, solitary, evidently straight. Mathias followed it for about two-thirds of a mile. Then its direction changed, leading the salesman left. The angle was rather obtuse—perhaps it was better not to reach the seashore too quickly. No side road, however, offered any alternative.

After scarcely ten minutes, he was once again on the main road at the crossroads. On the white milestone he read the freshly repainted directions: "Black Rocks Lighthouse—One Mile."

It was the usual kind of milestone: a rectangular parallelepiped flush with a half-cylinder of the same thickness (and with the same horizontal axis). The two principal sides—squares surmounted by half-circles—were inscribed with black characters; the rounded surface on top was shiny with new yellow paint. Mathias passed his hand in front of his eyes. He should have taken some aspirin before lunch. The headache that had dazed him since waking now began to make him suffer in earnest.

Mathias passed his hand in front of his eyes. He would ask his good friends the Mareks for some tablets. Another fifty yards and he turned—left—onto the road to the farm.

The landscape changed perceptibly: the higher embankment, which even obscured what was on either side of the road in some places, was lined with a virtually unbroken

hedge of thick bushes behind which rose the occasional
trunk of a pine tree. This far, at least, everything seemed
to be in order.

The treetops became more numerous. They were bent
and twisted in all directions with a general tendency, nevertheless, to yield to the prevailing winds—that is, to lean
toward the southeast. Some were lying practically on the
ground, raising only their dwarfed, irregular, almost leaf-
less tops.

The road did not continue beyond the farm, of which
the courtyard was its terminal enlargement.

In broad outline, there was little to describe again: the
sheds, the garden fence, the gray house with its clumps of
mahonia, the arrangement of the windows and the wide
expanse of bare stone above the door. . . . The whole picture corresponded almost perfectly to reality.

The salesman was walking forward on the beaten earth
floor which muffled the sound of his steps. The four windows were closed, but all the shutters were open—of course.
The only surprising thing about this house was the distance
between the two openings on the first floor. It looked as if
something were missing there—a niche, for instance, cut
into the wall to hold a statuette of the Virgin, or a wedding
bouquet under a glass bell, or some kind of mascot.

He was about to knock on the door panel when he noticed
that one of the mahonia bushes was about to die, if not
dead already; although the other bush was already showing
its buds, the one on the right bore only a few brownish
leaves at the ends of the stems, half-shriveled and spotted
with black.

The door was not bolted. Mathias pushed it open and
heard voices quite close by as he made his way down the
hallway—it sounded like a vehement argument. He stopped.

As soon as he had released it, the door slowly returned

to its original position without making the slightest sound. The kitchen door was ajar.

"Well? . . . Can't you say anything?"

"Oh, leave the boy alone. He told you he came straight here and waited for you out in the courtyard!"

That was the old country woman's voice. She sounded out of patience. Mathias took a step forward, carefully setting down his heavy shoe on the tiles. Through the opening, which was three or four inches wide, could be seen only one end of the table, covered with an oilcloth patterned with small, many-colored flowers, on which were lying a pair of glasses, a paper-knife, and two identical stacks of clean white plates, side by side; behind them, sitting bolt upright on a chair beneath a calendar tacked to the wall, was a young man holding himself perfectly motionless, his hands on his knees, head high, eyes fixed. He might have been fifteen or sixteen. Although his lips were not moving, it was easy to tell from his shiny, rigid face the importance of his role in this scene. Other people were talking and moving about in the rest of the room. Then came a man's voice: "He told me. . . . He told me! He was lying, as usual. Look at that mule's face. You think you know what's going on inside that head? The boy's not all there. . . . Still, he could answer a question when he's asked!"

"But he's told you again and again . . ."

"He sits there on that chair as if he had lost his tongue!"

"Because he's already told you what he had to say! You always start the same thing over and over."

"Oh, of course, I'm the one who's crazy!"

Heavy steps resounded on the cement, a man's steps (doubtless those of Robert Marek—who else could have been talking that way?). But nothing crossed Mathias' field of vision, the vertical strip remained unchanged: the cement squares of the floor, the table leg, the edge of the oilcloth with the pattern of little flowers, the steel-rimmed glasses, the long paper-knife with a black handle, the pile of four soup plates and the second pile just behind it, the upper part of the young man's body, a part of the back of his chair to the left, his frozen face, pinched mouth, fixed eyes, the illustrated calendar on the wall.

"If I knew he was the one who did it . . ." the father's voice growled.

The old woman began to cry. Amidst her wails and pleas for divine compassion, several words recurred again and again, a leitmotif: ". . . a murderer . . . murderer . . . he thinks his son is a murderer . . ."

"That's enough of that, Mother," the man shouted. The wailing stopped.

After a moment of silence, punctuated by the sound of his steps, he continued more deliberately: "You told us yourself that this—what did you call him?—this watch salesman had stopped here while I was away and found no one in the house. If Julian had been sitting on the doorstep, the way he claims he was, the man would certainly have seen him."

"He might have gone away for a minute . . . did you, darling?"

Mathias felt a sudden impulse to laugh, so unsuited to this impassive countenance was the word "darling," used by all the islanders in speaking to children. His efforts to contain himself prevented him from hearing an exchange in which he nevertheless made out a new voice—that of a younger woman. Yet the boy had not moved a muscle; perhaps these words did not really concern him after all, perhaps the others were interrogating someone else. This second feminine voice might be the boy's mother. . . . But no, she was away on a trip. Besides, the father had brutally silenced the importunate interruption; he continued his accusation: "First of all, Julian says he didn't leave the door. So he lied in any case. . . . The brat can't even keep his job in the bakery! Liar, thief, murderer! . . ."

"Robert! Are you crazy?"

"Yes, that's right—I'm the one who's crazy. . . .All right, you, are you going to answer—yes or no? You were out there, weren't you—out on the cliff, when that fellow came here; you had just time enough to get back before I did—without taking the road, since your grandmother didn't see you. . . . Well, say something, stubborn! You met the little Leduc girl, didn't you—you tried something with her? Oh, I know she wasn't a saint. . . . All you had to do was leave her alone. . . . And then? You were fighting? or what? Maybe you made her fall without meaning to? You were at the edge of the rock, and in the struggle. . . . Or was it for revenge, because they threw you off the pier the other night? Well? . . . You're going to say something or I'll break your head for you!"

"Robert, you're losing your temper again, you're . . ."

The salesman instinctively stepped back into the shadow: a sudden thrill of warmth ran through him. He realized that a change had just occurred (but when?) in the relation between the plates and the calendar, in the face directly opposite—now staring at his own. Immediately recovering his composure, Mathias walked deliberately toward the door, while the father's voice repeated louder and louder: "Then let him answer, let him answer!"

"Someone's there," the young man said.

Mathias exaggerated the noise his shoes made on the tiles and knocked with his ring on the half-open door. In the kitchen all sound had immediately ceased.

Then Robert Marek's voice said: "Come in!" and at the same moment the door was violently opened from inside. The salesman stepped forward. Everyone came toward him. They all seemed to know him: the old woman with the yellow face, the man in the leather jacket, even the young woman washing the dishes in a corner; half-turned toward the door, she had stopped in the midst of her work, a pot in her hand, and greeted him with a nod. Only the boy on the chair had not moved. He merely moved his eyes a little, in order to keep them fixed on Mathias.

Mathias, after having shaken all the hands held out to him, without succeeding despite his happy "hello's" in relaxing the tension in the air, ended up by walking over to the calendar tacked to the wall: "And there's Julian, my word! How he's grown! Let's see . . . how many years is it?"

"Can't you stand up when you're being spoken to?" shouted the father. "A real mule-face! That's why we were shouting a little, a minute ago: he's got himself fired from the bakery—yesterday morning—where he was working as an apprentice. I've half a mind to send him off as a cabin-boy if this goes on. . . . Always making trouble. . . . Last week he got into a fight with a drunken fisherman, fell in the harbor, and almost drowned. . . .That's what we were shouting about a minute ago. We were shaking some of the fleas out of him . . ."

Julian had stood up and was staring at his father. Then he turned and looked at the salesman. A vague smile hovered at the corners of his tightly-closed lips. He said nothing. Mathias did not dare hold out his hand to him. The wall was painted a flat ochre color of which the top layer was coming off here and there in polygonal scales. The picture on the calendar represented a little girl, her eyes blindfolded, playing blind-man's buff. He turned toward the grandmother: "And where are the children? I'd like to see them too . . ."

"They've gone back to school," Robert Marek said.

Julian's eyes did not leave the salesman's face, compelling him to speak, to speak rapidly, as rapidly as possible, in constant fear his mind would be wandering over dangerous ground, or into some place impossible to get out of . . . he had missed the boat last night; he came back to the farm because he thought he had forgotten something . . . (no). So he had to wait here until Friday; he would take advantage of his time to get some rest. Nevertheless, he had come back to the farm to sell one or two more watches . . .(no). He had missed the boat by about three minutes because of the bicycle he had rented, which at the last minute . . . (no); the chain had been giving him trouble since morning: when Madame Marek had seen him at the crossroads, at the fork, at the turn, he was already trying to get it back into place. Today, with plenty of time to spare, he was making the trip on foot; he was back at the farm to hear about the whole family . . .

"Did you bring your wrist watches with you?" the old country woman asked. Mathias was about to answer in the affirmative when he remembered he had left his suitcase with his landlady. He thrust his hand into his duffle coat pocket and brought out the only item he had with him: the little gold-plated lady's model returned this morning by . . .

"This is the only one I have left," he said, hoping to get out of the difficulty. Had not Madame Marek expressed the desire to furnish a certain member of her household with a watch—someone who was always late with her work?

The man in the leather jacket was not listening any more. At first, the old woman herself did not seem to understand; then her face brightened: "Ah, you mean Josephine!" she exclaimed, pointing at the girl. "No, she's not going to get any watch for a present—she'd forget to wind it. And she wouldn't know where she'd put it. And before three days were up she'd have lost it for good!"

The notion made both of them laugh. Mathias put the article back in his pocket. Deciding the situation was improving a little, he risked a glance in the young man's direction; but the latter had not moved, nor left off staring at Mathias. The father, who had been silent for several moments, suddenly asked the salesman point-blank: "I was sorry to get home too late yesterday to be able to see you. Do you happen to remember when it was you were here?"

"I'd say around noon," Mathias answered evasively.

Robert Marek looked at his son. "That's strange! And where were you at the time?"

A strained silence fell on the room again. Finally the boy decided to open his mouth. "I was in the shed on the other side of the courtyard," he said, without taking his eyes off the salesman.

"Yes," Mathias broke in hastily, "that's quite possible. I didn't see him because of the haystacks."

"There! You see!" cried the grandmother. "Just what I said all along!"

"What does that prove?" the man replied. "It's too easy to say that now!"

But the boy continued: "You got off the bicycle and you knocked at the door. Then you went to look at the gate to the garden. And before leaving you took a key out of a little bag fastened to the seat and used it to tighten something on your gearshift."

"Yes, that's right!" Mathias confirmed after each phrase, trying to smile as if these imaginary acts had been as obvious as they were unimportant.

All of which, in fact, merely reinforced his own alibi. Since Julian Marek was bearing witness to the fact that Mathias had been at the farm, had even waited some time for the absent owners, how could he have been on the cliff at the very moment—that is, in the opposite direction where the girl was tending her sheep? The salesman was obviously above suspicion from now on . . .

At least Mathias wanted to believe he was, with all his

might. Yet this unexpected guarantor disturbed rather than reassured him: he invented too glibly. If the boy had really been in the courtyard or the shed at the end of the morning, he knew perfectly well that no salesman had come to the door. On the other hand, if he hadn't been there and merely wanted to make his father think he had, why would he make up details as precise as the little bag, the key, and the gear-shift? The chances he would hit on the exact elements were so slight that their inventor ran the risk of an immediate and categorical denial. The only explanation—madness aside —would be that Julian had known beforehand that Mathias would not contradict him, in any case, because of his own irregular situation—because of his reciprocal fear of a denial.

Now, if Julian knew about the salesman's questionable status, it was obviously because he *had* been at the farm at the time of Mathias' supposed visit; he knew no one had knocked at the door. Which was why he had stared at the stranger so insolently at the very moment he was accumulating his fictitious details . . .

The question then remained the same as before: what was the boy's reason for supporting Mathias' position? Why, having told his father from the start that he had remained in the doorway, could he not defend himself against the declarations made by a passer-by to his grandmother? Was he afraid that the latter had a better chance of being believed than he himself?

No. From the moment Julian began lying—so recklessly— it seemed more likely that things had happened differently: the boy was not at the farm that morning. (On the other hand, he certainly was not in the hollow of the cliff—where he was accused of being; he was somewhere else, that was all.) And he believed the salesman had visited the farm. But since his father demanded actual proof, he had needed to invent some precise detail—hit upon by chance. In order

to ask Mathias' help—for he would think the whole matter
was of no importance to Mathias—Julian had looked him
straight in the eyes, hoping to communicate his distress and
obtain the salesman's complicity. What Mathias had attributed to insolence was really supplication. Or else the
young man was trying to hypnotize him . . .

All the way back down the little road, between the
gnarled trunks of the pines, the salesman examined the many
aspects of the problem over and over again. He reminded
himself that his headache might have prevented him from
arriving at a solution, for he would certainly have established
one indisputably if all his forces had been at his disposal.
In his haste to escape that inhospitable kitchen and the
young man's overinsistent stares, he had left without asking
for the aspirin tablets he had counted on. Words, efforts of
attention, all these calculations had now increased his discomfort to considerable proportions. He would be better
off having avoided that damned farm altogether.

On the other hand, wasn't it worth having provoked such
testimony? Julian Marek's public declaration, no matter
how confused his motives, nevertheless was the desired
proof that he had been waiting for some time in a place far
from the scene of the accident. . . . A place "far" from the
scene? Waiting for "some time"? How much time? As for
the distance, the whole island measured only four miles from
end to end! With a good bicycle . . .

After having struggled so hard to establish this alibi—
supposing it could free him from all suspicion—Mathias now
realized its inadequacy. He had stayed much too long on
the cliff to be able to account for his time in this manner.
There was still a hole in his schedule.

Mathias again began to recapitulate his movements since
leaving the café–tobacco shop–garage. It had been then
eleven-ten or eleven-fifteen. The distance to the Leduc

house being virtually negligible, his arrival there could be set at eleven-fifteen exactly. This first stop certainly accounted for less than fifteen minutes, although the woman's chatter had made it seem exasperatingly long. The subsequent stops had been both rare and brief—two or three minutes altogether. The mile or so on the main road, between town and the turn, at full speed and without a single side-trip, had taken scarcely more than five minutes. Five and three, eight; and fifteen, twenty-three. . . . Less than twenty-five minutes had therefore elapsed between his start at the square and the place where the salesman had encountered Madame Marek. That made it eleven-forty at the most, more likely eleven-thirty-five. Yet this meeting with the old country woman had actually occurred an hour later.

In order to reduce the difference as much as possible, Mathias tried getting back to the same point figuring backward from the moment he had looked at his watch (seven minutes after one) in the café at Black Rocks. He had been there about ten minutes, fifteen perhaps. It had taken ten minutes, at the most, for the second sale (to the exhausted-looking couple), and approximately fifteen for the first (including a long conversation with Madame Marek). This part of the road, traveled without any particular haste, might figure on the schedule as ten extra minutes. Unfortunately all these figures seemed a little excessive. Their total, nevertheless, scarcely exceeded three-quarters of an hour. The meeting with the old lady must therefore have occurred at twenty after twelve at the earliest—probably at twelve twenty-five.

The abnormal, excessive, suspicious, inexplicable time amounted to forty minutes—if not fifty. It was more than enough to account for the two successive detours: the trip to the farm and back—including the minor repair to the gearshift in front of the closed door—and the trip to the

cliff and back—including. . . . Mathias would merely have
had to hurry a little.

He hurried on. Then, having crossed the main road, he
continued down the opposite path—broad enough at the
outset but subsequently narrowing to a vague dirt track—
twisting to avoid roots and stumps, briar patches, and clumps
of stunted gorse. The fields had disappeared. The last wall
of fieldstone, half in ruins, indicated the beginning of the
road beyond. On either side stretched a series of low ridges
covered with reddish vegetation and relieved only occasionally by a gray rock, a thorn bush, or some vaguer, more
distant silhouette which was harder to identify—at first sight.

The terrain sloped down. Mathias noticed ahead of him,
at eye level, a darker line separating the uniform and motionless gray of the sky from another gray surface—similarly
flat and perpendicular—the sea.

The path came out onto the central section of a horseshoe-
shaped ridge facing the open sea, enclosing between its two
arms a kind of elongated basin which extended to the very
edge of the cliff, its dimensions not exceeding twenty by
thirty yards. A bright speck attracted the salesman's notice;
he was upon it in a few strides, and leaned over to pick it
up; it was only a tiny pebble, cylindrical, smooth, and white,
shaped deceptively like a cigarette.

The flattened bottom of the hollow, where the sparse
vegetation of the moor gave way to richer grass, came to
an end thirty steps away—without transition—in a steep rock
face, plunging down about fifteen yards into the eddying
water. After an almost perpendicular fall came an irregular
series of sharp, protruding ridges, and at the very base,
rising out of the foam between the more imposing rock
masses, a cluster of conical reefs against which the waves
dashed with great violence, countered by the backwash in

the opposite direction, producing bursts of spray that sometimes reached higher than the top of the cliff.

Higher still, two sea gulls described interlacing circles in the sky—sometimes executing them so that the loops occurred side by side, sometimes combining their circuits into a perfect figure eight—their maneuvers achieved without a single movement of their wings. The fixed, round eye which the slightly tilted head directed toward the interior of the horseshoe, stared immutably downward like the lidless eyes of fish, as if complete insensibility precluded any need to blink. He was watching the water rising and falling against the wet, polished rock, the runners of whitish moss, the periodic bursts of spray, the intermittent cascades, and farther away the rough stone outcroppings. . . . Suddenly Mathias noticed, a little to his right, a piece of cloth—knitted cloth—a piece of knitted gray wool hanging from a projecting rock two yards beneath the upper edge—that is, at a height the tide never reached.

Fortunately this spot looked accessible without too much difficulty. Without a moment's hesitation, the salesman took off his duffle coat, put it on the ground, and advanced along the edge of the precipice, making a detour of several yards to reach—still farther to the right—a point where the descent would be possible. From there, clinging with both hands to the outcroppings, moving his feet cautiously from fissure to projection, pressing his body against the granite flank, he reached, at the cost of more effort than he had supposed, not his goal but a point about two yards below it. Then he had only to stand up as high as he could, stretch out one arm (holding on with the other), and seize the desired object. The cloth came away from the rock without difficulty. There was no doubt about it, it was the gray sweater Violet had been wearing—had not been wearing, rather—but which had been lying on the grass beside her.

Yet Mathias was certain he had thrown it away with the rest, checking everything piece by piece to assure himself that nothing had caught on the rocks halfway down. It would have been better to leave the sweater at the top of the cliff in the hollow where the timid sheep were walking round and round their pickets. Since she had taken it off herself, it would have been more natural for her to fall without it. In any case, it seemed peculiar that she had lost her balance with it on, so that a projecting rock had stripped it from her as she fell without turning it inside out or even tearing it a little. It was lucky no one had discovered it during the search.

But at the same moment Mathias realized the uncertainty of such a conjecture, for the person who might have seen the sweater hanging there would doubtless not have risked trying to get it, regarding such an attempt as unnecessarily dangerous. Under such conditions would it not be a still graver error to remove it now? If someone had noticed it down there on the rock, would it not be better to put it back where he had found it, trying, in fact, to make it hang in exactly the same way?

Then, on consideration, Mathias wondered who such a witness might have been. Maria Leduc, discovering her sister's sweater, would certainly have decided she had fallen here, and brought a searching party in this direction, where no one had thought of looking yesterday. As for the fishermen who had found the body this morning, they had been down below, looking through the seaweed exposed at low tide, too far away to make out anything in particular. The compromising object had hitherto escaped notice.

Since, on the other hand, it was now impossible to put it back in the grassy hollow where Maria would have found it the day before, there remained only one solution. Mathias steadied himself by spreading his feet farther apart on the narrow ledge, wadded up the sweater into a compact mass, and grasping the rock wall behind him with one hand, threw the sweater out to sea with all his strength.

It landed gently on the water—floating between the rocks. The two gulls screamed, left off their circling, and plunged down together. They did not need to go as far as the water itself to recognize a simple piece of cloth, and immediately rose again, screaming still louder, toward the top of the cliff. Standing near the spot where he had left his duffle coat, at the edge of the vertical rock face, someone was leaning over the precipice, looking at the sea. It was young Julian Marek.

Mathias lowered his head so quickly that he almost fell in. At that moment the gray sweater, already half-saturated, was caught between a little wave and the backwash. Engulfed in the collision, it slowly sank, soon drawn out to sea beyond the rocks. When the surface rose again with the next wave, everything had disappeared.

Now he would have to raise his head toward the boy. The latter had obviously seen the sweater and the salesman's incomprehensible gesture. . . . No; he had certainly seen the gesture, but perhaps only a piece of gray cloth, wadded up into a ball. It was important to make him say just what it was he had seen.

Mathias also took into account his own bizarre position at the moment; he would have to furnish some explanation for that. He estimated the distance separating him from the cliff top. The silhouette against the sky frightened him all over again. He had almost forgotten its immediacy.

Julian watched him in silence with the same fixed eyes, thin lips, frozen features.

"Hey! Hello there, boy!" Mathias cried, pretending surprise, as if he had only then discovered his presence.

But the boy did not answer. He was wearing an old jacket over his work-clothes, and a cap that made him look older—at least eighteen. His face was thin, pale, and rather ominous.

"They thought I was throwing them a fish," the salesman said, pointing to the gulls spiraling over their heads. And he added, embarrassed by the persistent silence: "It was an old rag."

As he spoke he looked hard at the water moving under the parallel lines of foam between each wave. Nothing returned to the surface . . .

"A sweater."

The voice came from above, neutral, smooth, unchallengeable—the same voice which had said: "Before leaving you took a key out of a little bag fastened to the seat. . ." The salesman turned to face Julian. The latter's attitude and expression, or rather lack of expression, were exactly the same. It was as if he had never opened his mouth. "A sweater?" Had Mathias heard right? Had he heard anything?

Considering this distance of seven or eight yards, considering the noise of the wind and the waves (even though they were not so strong today), he could still manage to pretend he had not understood. His eyes swept over the gray wall again, examined the humps and hollows, then stopped in an indentation protected against the eddying waves, where the water level rose and fell more markedly along the polished surface of the rock.

"An old rag," he said. "I found it here."

"A sweater," corrected the voice of the imperturbable onlooker.

Although not shouting, he had spoken more loudly. No doubt remained. The same elements were repeated: the eyes raised toward the top of the cliff, the body leaning forward, the motionless face, the closed mouth. With a movement of his hand, Mathias specified: "Here, on the rocks."

"I know. It was there yesterday," the young man answered. And when Mathias had lowered his eyes: "It was Jackie's."

This time the salesman decided on an obvious interruption to give himself time to understand what was happening and to determine what line to take. He began climbing up the rocky slope by the same path he had taken down. It was much easier than the descent; he reached the top almost immediately.

But once on the moor at the cliff edge, he was still not certain what would be best to do. He walked as slowly as possible across the short distance still separating him from Julian Marek. What did he need to think about? Actually he had merely retreated before the threat, hoping, perhaps, that the other would say something more of his own accord.

Since the boy, on the contrary, maintained an obstinate silence, the salesman's first concern was to put his duffle coat back on. He thrust his hands into the pockets to check their contents. Nothing was missing.

"Smoke?" he asked, holding out the open pack of cigarettes.

Julian shook his head and stepped back. The salesman replaced the blue pack in his pocket, where his hand came in contact with the little cellophane bag.

"Would you like a gumdrop?" He held out the transparent bag filled with multicolored twists of paper.

The frozen face was already beginning to make the same sign of refusal, when the features underwent an almost imperceptible modification. Julian appeared to be changing his mind. He looked at the bag, then at the salesman, then at the bag again. It was at that moment that Mathias realized what was so extraordinary about his eyes: they expressed neither effrontery nor hostility, they were merely a little strabismic. The discovery reassured him.

Besides, Julian—now interested—was walking toward him to take a gumdrop out of the bag. Instead of taking the one on top, he pushed his fingers farther in, to grasp the twist of red paper he had decided on. He looked at it attentively, without unwrapping it. Then he looked at Mathias. . . . There was certainly some flaw in the young man's vision, yet he did not squint. It was something else. . . . Extreme myopia? No, he was holding the gumdrop at a normal distance from his eyes.

"Well, go on and eat it!" the salesman said, laughing at Julian's hesitation. Perhaps he was merely a little simple-minded.

The boy unbuttoned his jacket to reach one of the pockets in his work-clothes. Mathias thought he wanted to keep the tidbit for later.

"Here," he said, "take the whole bag."

"It's not worth it," Julian answered. And he stared again. . . . Could it have been a glass eye that made his stare so embarrassing?

"Is this yours?" the boy asked.

Mathias glanced from his eyes to his hands: the right one still held the wrapped gumdrop, and in the left, between thumb and forefinger, was an identical piece of red paper—shiny, translucent, crumpled—but untwisted and empty.

"It was here in the grass," Julian continued, with a movement of his head to indicate the little hollow beside them. "Is it yours?"

"Maybe I dropped it on the way," said the salesman, feigning indifference. He realized at once that gumdrop wrappers are not "dropped," but thrown away. To disguise his error he added, as agreeably as he could, "You can keep it too, if you like."

"It's not worth it," Julian answered.

The same quick smile he had noticed at the farm passed across the boy's thin lips. He wadded the rectangle of red paper into a hard ball and flicked it into the sea. Mathias followed its trajectory, but lost sight of it before it had reached the bottom of the cliff.

"What made you think it was mine?"

"It's just like those."

"What does that prove? I bought them in town. Anyone else could have bought them. Violet must have been eating them while she was tending the sheep . . ."

"Who is Violet?"

"I mean poor little Jacqueline Leduc. You're mixing me up with all your nonsense!"

The boy said nothing for several seconds. Mathias took advantage of the time to let his face become pleasant and peaceful again, a task he had not taken enough trouble with during the last few remarks. Julian took the gumdrop out of its wrapper and put it in his mouth; then he spat it out into his hand, wrapped the paper around it, and threw it into the sea.

"Jackie always bought caramels," he said afterward.

"Well, then it was someone else."

"At first you said it was you."

"Yes, it was. I took one just now, on the way here, and I threw the paper away. You're confusing me with your questions."

The salesman was talking naturally now, even cordially, as if he understood none of the reasons for this interrogation, but was nevertheless yielding to his interlocutor's childish caprices. One of the gulls plunged, then gained altitude with great strokes of its wings, almost grazing the two men as it passed them.

"I found it yesterday," Julian said.

Mathias, not knowing what to answer now, was on the point of walking away from young Marek with all the abruptness of justified impatience. Yet he remained where he was. Although it was impossible to prove anything by this one piece of red paper, it would be better not to alienate so persistent an investigator, one who might be acquainted with other elements of the story. But which ones?

There was already the episode of the gray sweater. Julian might also have discovered a second gumdrop wrapper—the green one—and the third half-smoked cigarette. . . . What else? The question of his presence at the farm at the time of the salesman's supposed visit also remained to be cleared up. Actually, if the boy had happened to be in the courtyard or the shed that morning, why had he not told his father that no one had knocked at the door? What was his motive in backing up Mathias' story? And if he had been somewhere else, why did he behave in such a strange way about it? After his long, stubborn silence, why this preposterous last-minute invention of a repair made to the bicycle gearshift? . . . A bolt tightened? . . . Perhaps that was the solution to all these incidents, now that he had come full circuit.

But if Julian Marek had not been at the farm, where had he been? Did his father have good reason for supposing him to have run off to the cliff on the way home from the bakery? Suddenly a wave of terror broke over Mathias: Julian, coming by another path—by "the other" path—to meet Violet, from whom he had demanded explanations—against whom, in fact, he harbored enough resentment to desire her death —Julian, catching sight of the salesman, had taken cover and had watched. . . . Mathias passed his hand over his forehead. Such imaginings did not hold water. His headache had become so violent that he was going out of his mind.

Was it not sheer madness to be ready—suddenly, because

of an ordinary gumdrop wrapper—to get rid of young Marek
by pushing him over the edge?

Until now Mathias had not taken into account the two
little pieces of paper which he had thrown away the day
before and which—to his mind, at least—did not constitute
actual evidence in the case. He considered it a matter of
bad taste that they should be so regarded, since he had not
even thought of recovering them; they had seemed so unimportant when he was in a state of composure. Julian himself had just unwrapped one quite casually, demonstrating
that nothing could be proved. . . . All the same, another
interpretation . . .

Another interpretation occurred to him: was this spec-
tacular gesture not meant to show that Julian would keep
silent, that the guilty party, once brought to light, would
have nothing to fear from *him*? His strange attitude back at
the farm could have no other explanation. There too he was
proclaiming his power over Mathias: he was destroying evidence with the same facility with which he unearthed further
indications of guilt, modifying as he chose the content of the
hours that had already elapsed. But there would have to be
something more than suspicions—even detailed suspicions—
to justify such assurance as this. Julian had "seen." There was
no use denying it any longer. Only the images registered by
these eyes could have given them such an intolerable fixity.

Yet they were quite ordinary gray eyes—neither ugly nor
beautiful, neither large nor small—two perfect, motionless
circles set side by side, each one pierced at the center by
a black hole.

The salesman had begun talking again to conceal his
agitation, rapidly and without a break—unconcerned, moreover, with relevance or even coherence; it did not seem to
matter much, since the boy was not listening. Any subject
he could think of seemed worth trying: the harbor shops,

the length of the crossing, the price of watches, electricity, the sound of the sea, the last two days' weather, the wind and the sun, the toads and the clouds. He also described how he had missed the return boat, which obliged him to remain on the island for several days; he was spending this compulsory leisure time, until his departure, making visits and taking long walks. . . . But when he came to a stop, out of breath, desperately casting about for something else to say in order not to repeat himself too much, he heard Julian's question, asked in the same neutral, even tone of voice: "Why did you go get Jackie's sweater again if you were only going to throw it into the sea?"

Mathias passed his hand over his forehead. Not "go get the sweater," but "go get the sweater again" . . . He began his answer in an almost supplicating tone: "Listen, boy, I didn't know it was hers. I didn't know it was anyone's. I only wanted to see what the gulls would do. You saw them: they thought I was throwing them a fish . . ."

The young man said nothing. He was looking Mathias straight in the eyes, his own fixed and strange—as if unconscious, even blind—or imbecile.

And Mathias still went on talking, though without the slightest conviction, carried away by the flood of his own words across the deserted moor, across the series of dunes where no trace of vegetation remained, across the rubble and the sand, darkened here and there by a sudden shadow of a specter forcing him to retreat. He went on talking. And the ground, from sentence to sentence, gave way a little more beneath his feet.

He had come out here on one of his strolls, following the paths wherever they led, for no other reason than to stretch his legs a little. He had noticed a piece of cloth hanging from the rocks. Having climbed down to have a look, out of sheer curiosity, he had decided it was merely an old rag of no possible use (but Julian was doubtless aware of the gray sweater's excellent condition . . .) and had unthinkingly thrown it to the gulls to see what they would do. How could he have known that this rag, this dirty piece of wool (on the contrary, extremely clean)—this object, really—belonged to little Jacqueline? He didn't even know this was the place she had fallen . . . fallen . . . fallen. . . . He stopped. Julian was looking at him. Julian was going to say: "She didn't fall, either." But the boy did not open his mouth.

The salesman resumed his monologue still more rapidly. It was no easy matter to climb down the rocks, especially wearing such big shoes. Toward the top the ground might easily cave in under his feet. Yet he hadn't suspected it was so dangerous; otherwise he would not even have tried. Since he didn't know this was the place. . . . But no one had said any such thing; the fact that the sweater belonged to Jacqueline did not mean the accident had occurred here. Just now, in the matter of the gumdrop wrapper, Mathias had already given himself away, admitting he knew the exact spot where the girl tended her sheep. Too late, now, to go back. . . . He couldn't suppose, in any case, given the position of the sweater, that it had been torn off in the course of her fall . . . etc.

"That's not it, either," said Julian.

Mathias was seized with panic and hurried on, too apprehensive for explanations. He began to speak at such a rate that objections—or even regret at his own words—became utterly impossible. In order to fill in the blanks, he often repeated the same sentence several times. He even caught himself reciting the multiplication table. Seized with a sudden inspiration, he fumbled in his pocket and brought out the little gold-plated wrist watch: "Here, since it's your birthday I'm going to give you a present: look at this fine watch!"

But Julian, his eyes still fixed on Mathias', retreated farther and farther into the grassy hollow, away from the edge of the cliff toward the curve of the horseshoe. Lest the boy run away even faster, the salesman dared not make the least move in his direction. He stood where he was, holding in his outstretched hand the watch with its band of metal links, as if he were trying to tame birds.

When he reached the foot of the slope bordering the inner limit of the horseshoe, the young man stopped, his eyes still fixed on Mathias'—who was equally motionless, twenty yards away.

"My grandmother will give me a finer one," he said.

Then he thrust his hand into his work-clothes and brought out a handful of miscellaneous fragments, among which the salesman recognized a thick cord spotted with grease; it seemed washed out or discolored, as if by prolonged immersion in sea water. The other things were hard to see at this distance. Julian picked out a cigarette butt—already three-quarters smoked—and put it between his lips. The little cord and the other articles went back into his pocket. He buttoned his jacket again.

Keeping the butt in the right corner of his mouth—without lighting it—and his glassy eyes on the salesman, the boy waited, his face pale; the brim of his cap was tilted slightly toward his left ear. Mathias lowered his eyes first.

"You rented the new bicycle from the tobacco shop," the voice said next. "I know that bike. There's no tool bag under the seat. The tools are in a box behind the luggage rack." Of course. The salesman had noticed it right away the day before: a chromium-plated, rectangular box—one of the permanent accessories; on its rear surface was the red reflector, usually attached to the mudguard. Of course.

Mathias lifted his head again. He was alone on the moor. In front of him, in the grass, in the center of the little hol-

low, he saw a short cigarette butt—which Julian must have
thrown away as he was leaving—or else it was the one he
had been looking for himself since morning—or perhaps they
were one and the same. He came closer. It was only a little
pebble, cylindrical, white, and smooth, which he had already
picked up once, when he had come here.

Mathias headed slowly toward the big lighthouse, taking
the customs road along the edge of the cliff. He could not
help laughing at the thought of the dramatic retreat Julian
had just made in order to reveal his discovery: a metal box
fastened behind the luggage rack. . . . The salesman had
never denied it! Was this detail so important that he ought
to have corrected Julian when he spoke of a bag under the
seat? If he had no proof better than that. . .

He might just as well have said that the gray sweater was
not lying "on the rocks," but "on a projection of the rocks"—
or that only one of the mahonias was budding at the Marek
farm. He might have said: "The road is not altogether level,
nor entirely straight, between the crossroads and the fork
leading to the mill"—"The bulletin-board is not precisely in
front of the café–tobacco shop door, but slightly to the right,
and does not block the entrance"—"The little square is not
really triangular: the apex is flattened by the plot of grass
around the public building so as to form a trapezoid"—"The
enameled iron skimmer sticking out of the mud in the harbor
is not the same color blue as the one in the hardware store"
—"The pier is not rectilinear, but turns in the center at an
angle of one hundred seventy-five degrees."

Similarly the time wasted at the crossroads to the Marek
farm did not amount to forty minutes. The salesman had
not arrived there before eleven-forty-five or eleven-fifty,
taking into account the long detour to the mill. On the other
hand, before meeting up with the old country woman at
twelve-twenty, he had spent nearly fifteen minutes repair-

ing the gearshift on his bicycle—with the help of the tools
that were in the box . . . etc. There remained just enough
time to make the trip to the farm and back—including the
wait in the courtyard, near the mahonia bush, and the first
two attempts to deal with the abnormal friction of the
chain: on the little path, then in front of the house.

The customs road did not actually follow the edge of the
cliff very closely—at least not continuously—and often di-
verged from it for three or four yards, sometimes for much
greater distances. Besides, it was not easy to determine
where this "edge" actually was, for with the exception of
the areas where a steep rock wall towered above the sea
for the whole height of the cliff, there were also grassy
slopes running down almost to the water, as well as heaps
of jagged rock more or less encroaching on the moor, and
even planes of schist that ended in huge lumps of rubble
and earth.

Sometimes the indentations along the shore were enlarged
by a deep fault cutting into the cliff, or a sandy bay forming an even larger jag. The salesman had been walking for
a long time—it seemed to him—when the lighthouse suddenly rose up before him, high above the mass of auxiliary
constructions, walls and turrets clustered together.

Mathias turned left, toward the village. A man in fisherman's clothes had been walking ahead of him on the road
for some time now. Following him, Mathias again came out
onto the main road where the first houses began, and walked
into the café.

There were many people, much smoke and noise. The
electric lights hanging from the ceiling had been turned
on; they were harsh and blue. Scraps of almost incomprehensible conversation were momentarily audible in the general
uproar; here and there a gesture, a face, a grin emerged
from the shimmering haze for a few seconds.

There was no table free. Mathias headed toward the bar. The other customers pressed a little closer together to make room for him. Exhausted by his day's walking, he would have preferred to sit down.

The fat, gray-haired woman recognized him. He had to make explanations all over again: the boat he had missed, the bicycle, the bedroom . . . etc. The proprietress, fortunately, had too much to do to listen or question him. He asked her for some aspirin. She had none. He ordered an absinthe. Besides, his headache was bothering him less now; it had become a sort of cottony humming in which his whole brain was steeped.

An old man next to him was telling a story to a group of the lighthouse workmen. They were young, and laughed at him, or nudged one another with their elbows, or else interrupted with bantering, apparently serious observations which produced still more laughter. The narrator's low voice was lost in the din. Only a few phrases, a few words reached Mathias' ears. Nevertheless, he understood, as a result of the old man's deliberation and his incessant repetitions, as well as from the sarcastic remarks of his listeners, that he was telling an old local legend—which Mathias had never heard mentioned in his childhood, however: each spring, a young virgin had to be hurled from the top of the cliff to appease the storm-god and render the sea kind to travelers and sailors. Rising from the deep, a gigantic monster with the body of a serpent and the head of a dog devoured the victim alive under the eyes of the sacrificer. It was doubtless the little shepherdess' death that had provoked such a story. The old man furnished a quantity of mostly inaudible details about the ceremony; it was strange that he used only the present tense: "they make her kneel down," "they tie her hands behind her back," "they blindfold her," "down in the water they can see the slimy coils of the dragon" . . . A fisherman slipped in between Mathias and the group of men to reach the counter. The salesman squeezed in the opposite direction. Now he could hear nothing but the young men's exclamations and laughter.

". . . little Louis was mad at her too . . . their engagement . . . had threatened her . . ." This voice was loud and sententious; it came from the opposite direction, over the heads of three or four drinkers.

Behind Mathias, several people were still discussing the recent sensation. The whole room, the whole island, was passionately interested in the tragic accident. The fat woman served the newcomer on the salesman's left a glass of red wine. She was holding the bottle in her left hand.

On the wall, above the top row of apéritifs, hung a yellow placard attached by four tacks: "Buy your watch at your jeweler's."

Mathias finished his absinthe. No longer feeling the little suitcase between his legs, he lowered his eyes toward the floor. The suitcase had disappeared. He thrust his hand into his duffle coat pocket to rub his grease-spotted fingers against the wad of cord, keeping his eyes fixed on the salesman. The proprietress thought he was looking for change and shouted out the price of his drink; but it was the absinthe he was going to pay for. He turned to face the fat woman, or the woman, or the girl, or the young barmaid, then set down the suitcase in order to pick up the suitcase while the sailor and the fisherman sneaked between, crept between, came between, Mathias and the salesman . . .

Mathias passed his hand over his forehead. It was almost night now. He was sitting in a chair in the middle of the street—in the middle of the road—in front of the Black Rocks café.

"Feeling better now?" asked a man wearing a leather jacket.

"Much better, thank you," Mathias answered. He had already seen this person somewhere. He wanted to justify his indisposition, and said, "It's the smoke, the noise, so much talk . . ." He could not find words to express himself. Yet he stood up with no difficulty.

He glanced around for the suitcase, but immediately remembered he had left it in his room that morning. He thanked the man again and picked up the chair to return it to the café, but the man took it out of his hands, and the only thing left for the salesman to do was to leave—by the road to the solitary cottage in its reed-filled valley at the back of the narrow cove.

In spite of the half-darkness, he walked on unhesitatingly. When the path followed the edge of the cliff, above the sea, he felt no fear whatsoever, although scarcely making out where he was putting his feet. With sure steps he climbed down toward the house, where a single, curtainless window showed a reddish gleam in the blue twilight.

He bent his head toward the panes. Despite the accumulated dust clinging to the surface, what was happening inside could be seen quite clearly. It was rather dark, especially in the corners. Only the objects near the source of light were really clear to Mathias—who was standing sufficiently far back to remain invisible to anyone inside.

The scene is lit by an oil lamp in the middle of the long, blackish-brown table. Also on the table, between the lamp and the window, are two white plates next to each other—touching each other—and an uncorked liter bottle of which the dark glass prevents any certainty as to the color of the liquid filling it. The rest of the table is clear, marked only with a few shadows: the huge, distorted one cast by the bottle, a crescent underlining the plate nearest the window, a large spot surrounding the lamp base.

Behind the table, in the room's right corner (the one

farthest away), the big kitchen stove against the rear wall can be discerned by an orange glow from the open ash-drawer.

Two people are standing face to face: Jean Robin—called Pierre—and, much shorter than he, the young woman of unknown identity. Both are on the other side of the table (in relation to the window), he to the left—that is, in front of the window—she at the opposite end of the table, near the stove.

Between them and the table—running its whole length but concealed from view by it—is the bench. The entire room is thus cut up into a network of parallel lines: first the back wall, against which, at the right, are the stove and several boxes, and at the left, in shadow, some more important piece of furniture; next, at an unspecifiable distance from this wall, the line determined by the man and the woman; then, still advancing toward the front of the room, the invisible bench, the central axis of the rectangular table—including the oil lamp and the opaque bottle—and the window itself.

Cutting across this system by perpendiculars, from front to back, the following elements can be discerned: the central upright of the window, the shadow crossing the second plate, the bottle, the man (Jean Robin, or Pierre), a crate set upright on the floor; then, a yard to the right, the lighted oil lamp; and about a yard farther, the end of the table, the young woman of unspecified identity, and the left side of the stove.

Two yards—or a little more—separate the man from the woman. She lifts her timorous face toward him.

At this moment the man opens his mouth, moving his lips as if talking, but nothing can be heard by the observer behind the square panes. The window is too tightly closed; or the noise of the sea behind him, breaking against the reef at the mouth of the cove, is too loud. The man does not articulate his words clearly enough for the syllables to be counted. He has been speaking slowly for some ten seconds—which must be about thirty syllables, perhaps less.

In reply the young woman screams something—four or five syllables—at the top of her lungs, it appears. Yet this time too, nothing can be heard through the glass. Then she steps forward toward the man and rests one hand (the left) on the edge of the table.

Now she is looking at the lamp and says a few words more —less intensely—as her features become progressively more distorted and a grimace narrows her eyes, widens the corners of her mouth, and raises the wings of her nostrils.

She is crying. A tear can be seen falling slowly down her cheek. The girl sits down on the bench; without putting her legs between it and the table, she turns the upper part of her body toward the latter and rests her forearms on it, hands clasped. Finally she lets her head droop forward, her face hidden in her hands. Her golden hair gleams in the lamplight.

Then the man slowly approaches, stands behind her, stares at her for a moment, stretches out his hand, and slowly caresses the nape of her neck with his fingertips. The huge hand, the blond head, the oil lamp, the edge of the first plate (on the right), and the left upright of the window are all aligned in the same oblique plane.

The lamp is made of brass and clear glass. From its square base rises a cylindrical, fluted stem supporting the oil reservoir—a half-globe with its convexity underneath. This reservoir is half-full of a brownish liquid which does not resemble commercial oil. On its upper part is a flange of stamped metal an inch and a half high, into which is screwed the glass—a perpendicular tube widening slightly at the base. It is this perforated flange, brightly lighted from with-

in, which can be seen most clearly of all the articles in the
room. It consists of two superimposed series of equal tangent
circles—rings, more exactly, since their centers are hollow—
each ring of the upper series being exactly above a ring of
the lower row to which it is joined for a fraction of an inch.

The flame itself, produced from a circular wick, appears
in profile in the form of a triangle deeply scalloped at the
apex, therefore exhibiting two points rather than just one.
One of these is much higher than the other, and sharper as
well; the two joints are united by a concave curve—two
asymmetrical, ascending branches on each side of a rounded
depression.

Blinded from staring at the lamp too long, Mathias finally
turned away his eyes. To rest them, he examined the window itself—four identical panes with neither curtain nor
shade, looking out into the darkness of the night. He blinked
violently several times, pressing his eyeballs in order to get
rid of the circles of fire still printed on his retinas.

He brought his head close to the glass and tried to look
through, but could see nothing: neither sea nor moon nor
even the garden. There was no sign of the moon or the
stars—the darkness was complete. Mathias returned to his
memorandum book, open at the day's date—Wednesday—on
the massive little table wedged into the window recess.

He re-read the schedule he had just brought up to date,
accounting for his recent movements. For the day that had
just passed, on the whole, there was little to suppress, or to
add. And besides, he had met too many witnessess.

He turned back a leaf, found himself at Tuesday, and
once again went over the imaginary succession of minutes
between eleven in the morning and one in the afternoon.
He confined himself to closing the ill-formed loop of an
eight with the point of his pencil. Everything else was in
order.

But he smiled, thinking of the futility of his task. Such a concern for exactitude—unaccustomed, excessive, suspect—far from clearing him, rather tended to accuse. . . . In any case, it was too late. Young Julian Marek had probably turned him in late that afternoon. Certainly after their encounter at the edge of the cliff the boy's doubts had vanished completely; the salesman's words and ridiculous behavior gave him away indisputably, without even taking into account what Julian knew already, perhaps from having seen it with his own eyes. Tomorrow, early in the morning, the old Civil Guard would come to arrest "the unspeakable individual who . . . ," etc. There was no hope of escaping in a fishing boat: the police in all the little mainland harbors would be waiting for him as he arrived.

He wondered if they used handcuffs on the island, and how long the chain linking the two rings would be. On the right side of the memorandum book were listed amounts received, as well as descriptions of articles sold. This part, at least, had needed no retouching, and showed no flaws, since Mathias had recovered possession of the wrist watch given away the day before. He decided to finish the account of this unjustified day: at the top of Wednesday's page he wrote two words, pressing hard on the pencil: "slept well."

On Thursday's page—still blank—he wrote in advance the same remark. Then he closed the black book.

He set the oil lamp on the pedestal table at the head of his bed, undressed, piling his clothes on the chair, put on the nightshirt his landlady had lent him, wound his watch and laid it near the lamp base, lowered the wick a little, and blew into the top of the chimney.

While he was groping for the open side of the bedsheets, he remembered the electric light. When the latter had suddenly gone out he had flicked the switch back and forth several times, supposing that the circuit was in bad working order. But the light had not come back on despite all his manipulations, and soon the landlady was knocking at his door (with her foot?), holding a lighted oil lamp in each hand. The "local breakdowns," she said, were very frequent and sometimes lasted a long time; the islanders had therefore retained their old oil lamps, which they kept ready for use as in the past.

"It wasn't worth making all that fuss about progress," the woman had concluded, carrying away only one of her two lamps.

Mathias did not know in which position he had left the switch. If it was "off," then the current might have been reestablished for some time now without his knowing it; and on the other hand, the light might suddenly go on in the middle of the night. He reached the door in the darkness, his hands recognizing as he passed them the chair with his clothes on it and the marble top of the big commode.

He flicked the switch near the door. There was still no current. Mathias tried to remember which position was "off," but could not, and pressed the little metallic ball for a last time, just in case.

Groping his way back to bed, he slipped between the sheets which seemed cold and damp. He stretched out on his back at full length, legs together, arms crossed over his chest. His left hand bumped into the wall. The outlines of the window on his right began to emerge from the darkness —a vague, dark blue gleam.

It was only then that the salesman realized how tired he was—overcome by an immense fatigue. The last mile or so, taken at a fast pace in the dark from Black Rocks to town had exhausted his strength. At dinner he had scarcely touched the food the proprietor had served him; fortunately the latter did not speak to him once. Mathias had hurried through the meal in order to return to his room—the back room with the high, dark furniture—looking out onto the moor.

Thus he was alone again in this room where he had spent his whole childhood—with the exception, of course, of his first years following his mother's death, which had occurred shortly after his birth. His father had remarried soon after, and had immediately taken Mathias back from his aunt, who had intended to bring him up as her own son. The child, adopted quite naturally by the new bride, had spent a long time wondering which of the two women was his mother; it had taken him still longer to understand that he had no mother at all. He had often heard the story before.

He wondered if the big corner cupboard, between the door and the window, was still locked. That was where he had kept his string collection. It was all over now. He did not even know where the house was anymore.

At the foot of the bed, on the chair with its back against the wall (where a horizontal streak had been worn into the wallpaper), sat Violet, a timorous expression on her face. The childish chin was pressed against the rail of the wooden bed, around which her little hands were clasped. Behind her was another cupboard, a third one on the right, then the dressing table, two other chairs different in design from each other, and finally the window. He was alone again in this room where he had spent his whole life, looking through the curtainless panes of the small, square window set deep in the wall. It looked out over the moor, with no courtyard or even the least bit of a garden intervening. Twenty yards from the house stood a big wooden fence post—the remains of something, no doubt; on its rounded extremity was perched a sea gull.

The sky was gray and the wind came in strong gusts. Yet the gull remained completely motionless on its perch. It could have been there a long time; Mathias had not seen it come.

Its head was facing toward the right, in profile. It was a big whitish bird with no dark patch on its head; its wings were of a darker color, though they looked dusty: it was a common species.

It is a big gray and white bird; its head has no dark patch. Only the wings and tail have any color. It is the type of sea gull most common in the vicinity.

Mathias has not seen it come. It must have been there a long time, motionless on its perch.

Its head is facing toward the right, in profile. The points of the long, folded wings cross over the tail, which is rather short. The beak is horizontal, thick, yellow, slightly curved, but strongly hooked at the tip. Darker feathers border the lower edge of the wing as well as its sharp tip.

The right leg (the only one visible, the left being directly behind it) is a thin vertical stem covered with yellow scales. It begins, under the belly, with a joint attached at an angle of one hundred twenty degrees, connecting at one end with the fleshy, feathered part just the beginning of which can be distinguished. At the other end of the leg can be seen the webbing between the toes and the pointed claws spread out on the rounded extremity of the fence post.

From this post is hung the wicket-gate connecting the moor with the garden, which is surrounded by a barbed-wire fence attached to wooden posts. The garden, carefully laid out in parallel beds separated by well-kept lanes, is a profusion of many-colored blossoms sparkling in the sunshine.

Mathias opens his eyes. He is in his bed, lying on his back. In the half-consciousness of waking, the bright (but vague) image of the window, now on his left, begins to move around the room with an irresistible although uniform movement, as steady and deliberate as the current of a river, appearing successively at the places which should be occupied by the chair at the foot of the bed, the cupboard, the second cupboard, the dressing table, the two chairs side by side. Then the window stops at Mathias' right—at the place it occupied yesterday—four identical panes divided by a dark cross.

It is broad daylight. Mathias has slept well, not waking once, not moving an inch. He feels rested, calm. He turns his head toward the window.

It is raining outside. The sun was shining in his dream. He suddenly remembers it for a second, after which it immediately disappears.

It is raining outside. The four panes are spattered with tiny brilliant drops forming oblique—although parallel—lines less than half an inch long, cross-hatching the window's whole surface in the direction of one of its diagonals. The almost imperceptible sound of the raindrops against the glass is audible.

The lines occur closer and closer together. Soon the fusion of the drops with one another disturbs the well-ordered pattern. The shower was just beginning when Mathias turned his eyes toward the window. Now big drops are forming everywhere, streaming along the glass from top to bottom.

Threads of water cover the whole image, their direction generally vertical, a series of winding lines occurring at regular intervals of about three-eighths of an inch.

These vertical threads disappear in their turn, giving way to a punctuation with neither direction nor movement—thick, frozen drops evenly covering the whole surface. Each of these, observed attentively, reveals a different, although uncertain, form in which only a single constant characteristic is preserved: the swollen, rounded base shading into black and touched at the center with a speck of light.

At this moment Mathias notices that the electric light hanging from the ceiling (in the middle of the room between the window and the bed) is on, shining with a yellow radiance at the end of its wire beneath a lamp shade of ground glass that has a rippled edge.

He stands up and goes to the door. There he flicks the chromium switch fastened to the door frame. The light goes out. For the light to be off the little polished metal ball must be in the "down" position—how logical. Mathias should have thought of that last night. He looks at the floor, then at the oil lamp on the pedestal table.

The tiles feel cold under his bare feet. About to get back into bed, he turns around, walks to the window, and leans over the table wedged into the recess. The liquid granulations covering the panes on the outside are impossible to see through. Although wearing only his nightshirt, Mathias opens the window.

It is not cold. It is still raining, but only a little; and there is no wind. The sky is uniformly gray.

Nothing remains of the sudden squall that drove the rain against the panes a few moments before. The weather is very calm now. A continuous light rain is falling; if it blurs the horizon it does not obstruct the view for shorter distances. On the contrary, it is as if in this new-washed air the objects near at hand profit from an additional luster— especially when they are light-colored to begin with—like that gull, for instance, arriving from the southeast (where the cliff falls away to the sea). Its already deliberate flight seems to become even slower as it loses altitude.

After turning around almost in the same place, in front of the window, the gull slowly rises again. But then it lets itself drop to the ground without once beating its wings, in a short, sure, widening spiral.

Instead of landing, the gull rises again, effortlessly, merely by changing the inclination of its wings. Then it turns once again, as if it were looking for its prey, or a perch—twenty yards from the house. It gains altitude with a few great strokes of its wings, describes a last loop, and continues its flight toward the harbor.

Mathias returns to his bed and begins to dress. After a summary toilet he puts on the rest of his clothes: the jacket and the duffle coat as well, since it is raining. He automatically thrusts his hands into the pockets. But he pulls out the right hand at once.

He heads toward the big cupboard in the corner, next to the window, between the chairs and the desk. The two doors are closed tight. The key is not in the keyhole. He opens one door with his fingertips—it opens easily. The cupboard was not locked. He opens it wide. It is absolutely empty. On the entire surface of its great, regularly-spaced shelves there is not even the smallest piece of cord.

The desk at the left of the cupboard is not locked either. Mathias drops the leaf in front, opens the many drawers one after another, inspects the pigeonholes. Here too everything is empty.

The five big drawers of the commode on the other side of the door can be opened just as easily, although they have no handles, merely wide openings of old—missing—locks into which Mathias thrusts the tip of his little finger in order to draw them toward him, getting a purchase on the wood as well as he can. But from top to bottom of the commode he finds nothing: not one piece of paper, not one old box top, not one piece of string.

He picks up his watch from the pedestal table next to him and fastens it around his left wrist. It is nine o'clock.

He crosses the room to where the memorandum book is lying on the square table in the window recess. He opens it to Thursday, picks up his pencil, and under the indication "slept well" adds in his most painstaking handwriting: "up at nine"—although he is unaccustomed to recording such details as this.

Then he stoops, seizes the little suitcase under the table, and puts the black memorandum book in it. After a moment's reflection he puts the suitcase on the lowest shelf of the big empty cupboard in the right corner.

Having closed the door—forcing it a little in order to make it stay closed—he automatically thrusts his hands into his duffle coat pockets. The right hand again comes in contact with the gumdrops and the cigarettes. Mathias removes one of the latter from the pack and lights it.

He takes his wallet from his inside jacket pocket, removes a small newspaper clipping whose edge protrudes slightly beyond the other papers inside. He reads this printed text from beginning to end, chooses a word in it, and after tapping the ash from his cigarette, brings the red tip near the selected spot. The paper immediately turns brown. Mathias gradually presses harder. The brown spot spreads; the cigarette finally burns through the paper, leaving a round hole ringed with black.

Then, with the same deliberation and care, Mathias pierces a second identical hole at a certain distance from the first. Between them is only a thin blackened isthmus, scarcely a thirty-second of an inch wide at the point of tangency between the two circles.

New holes succeed these two, first grouped in pairs, then occurring in whatever space is left. The rectangle of newspaper is soon entirely perforated. Mathias then undertakes to make it disappear altogether, gradually burning whatever fragments remain with his cigarette. He begins at one corner and proceeds along the fuller parts of the lacework, taking care that no piece falls off unless it is a completely charred fragment. When he blows gently at the point of contact he notices that the line of incandescence gains ground a little more quickly. From time to time he inhales on the cigarette to quicken combustion of the tobacco; he knocks the ashes onto the tiles at his feet.

When nothing is left of the clipping but a tiny triangle which he holds between the points of two fingernails, Mathias sets this fragment on the floor, where he finishes it off. Thus no trace of the news item discernible to the naked eye remains. The cigarette itself has diminished, during the course of the operation, to a half-inch butt which it is only natural to toss out the window.

Mathias gropes at the bottom of his pocket for the two overlong butts he had recovered in the grass on the cliff top. He lights them one after the other in order to reduce them to a less noticeable size; he smokes them as rapidly as possible, inhaling puff after puff, and throws them in turn out the window.

His right hand again plunges into the pocket, this time bringing out a gumdrop. The transparent wrapper goes back into the bag while the brownish cube is put into his mouth. It is rather like a caramel.

Mathias buttons up his duffle coat. Since there is no wind, it will probably not rain in; no need to close the window. Mathias walks over to the door.

The moment he opens it to step into the hallway and cross the house—since the main entrance is on the other side—he decides that his landlady, if he should meet her, will doubtless want to talk to him. He leaves the door of his room ajar, making no noise. Some indistinct words reach him, probably from the kitchen at the other end of the hallway. Among several voices he recognizes his landlady's. Two men—at least—are talking with her. It sounds as if they were trying not to raise their voices—as if they were even whispering from time to time.

Mathias closes the door carefully and turns back to the window. It is very easy to get out that way. Having hoisted himself up on the heavy little table, kneeling in order not to scratch the waxed wood, he straddles the sill, crouches on the outer stone ledge, and jumps down into the low grass of the moor. If the two men want to talk to him, they can just as well do it later on.

Mathias walks straight ahead; the moist air refreshes his forehead and his eyes. The carpetlike vegetation along this part of the coast is so full of water that the soles of his shoes sound like sponges being squeezed. Walking on this elastic, half-liquid soil is easy and spontaneous—whereas last night his feet were constantly bumping into invisible stones along the way. This morning, all the salesman's fatigue has vanished.

He reaches the edge of the cliff almost immediately; it is quite low in this area. The tide is still ebbing. The sea is perfectly calm. The regular hiss of the waves is scarcely louder than the sound of his shoes in the grass, but slower. To the left can be seen the long, rectilinear pier sticking out at an angle toward the open sea, and at its tip the beacon-light turret indicating the entrance to the harbor.

Continuing in this direction, sometimes on the moor, sometimes on the rocks themselves, Mathias' progress is hindered by a long crevice running perpendicular to the shoreline. It is no more than a yard wide at the top, narrowing below until it is too restricted for anything larger than the body of a child to slip through. But the crevice must penetrate much deeper into the rock; the various outcroppings along the sides make it impossible to see to the bottom. Instead of widening as it approaches the sea, the crevice narrows still more—at least on the surface—and offers, along the cliffside, no practicable opening in the chaos of granite blocks extending as far as the beach. It is therefore impossible to slip into it at any point.

Mathias takes the bag of gumdrops out of his pocket, opens it, inserts a pebble for ballast, twists the cellophane neck several times, and drops it where the crevice seems least choked. The object bumps against the stone sides once, then again, but without being damaged or obstructed in its fall. Then it disappears from sight, swallowed by distance and darkness.

Leaning over the crevice, his ears straining, Mathias hears it ricochet a third time against something hard. A characteristic noise, immediately afterward, indicates that the body has ended its course in a hole full of water. The latter doubtless communicates with the open sea at high tide, but by channels too narrow and complicated for the undertow ever to bring the little bag to light. Mathias straightens up, makes a detour in order to bypass the crevice, and continues his interrupted walk. He wonders if crabs like gumdrops.

Soon the flat rocks on which the beginning of the big pier is constructed are at his feet—sloping reaches of gray stone that extend to the water without the least bit of beach, even at low tide. Here the customs path joins a more important road to the interior, turning away from the shore at an old, half-razed wall, apparently the remains of the ancient royal city.

Mathias climbs down the rocks without difficulty, owing to their convenient arrangement. In front of him rises the outer wall of the pier, extending vertically and rectilinearly toward the beacon light.

He climbs down the last slope, then up the few steps leading to the quay by the opening cut into the massive parapet. He finds himself once again on the rough pavement,

new-washed by the morning's rain. The harbor is as smooth
as a frozen pond: not the slightest undulation, not the slightest ripple at the edge, not the slightest tremor on the surface.
At the end of the pier, moored against the landing slip, a
small trawler is loading crates. Three men—two on the pier,
one on the deck—laboriously pass them from hand to hand.

The strip of mud exposed below the quay no longer looks
the same as on the preceding days. Mathias nevertheless has
to think several seconds before he realizes the nature of the
change, for nothing strikes the eye as extraordinary in this
grayish-black expanse: it is merely "clean"—all the debris
which previously covered it has been removed at one stroke.
Mathias actually recalls having noticed, the day before, a
group of men raking here at low tide. The proprietor had
remarked that certain habits of cleanliness had been maintained on the island ever since the naval occupation. The
salesman had pretended, of course, to remember something
of the kind from his earliest childhood; but in reality he had
completely forgotten this detail, along with all the rest, and
such images awakened no response.

Remains of shellfish, pieces of iron or crockery, half-rotten
seaweed—everything has disappeared. The sea has smoothed
out the layer of mud, and as it retreats, leaves behind a shining, immaculate beach from which emerge here and there
only a few solitary rounded stones.

As soon as he enters the café, the proprietor calls out to
Mathias; there is a chance for him to return to the city without waiting for the boat tomorrow night. A trawler—the one
at the landing slip—will be leaving in a little while for the
mainland; in spite of the strict regulations, the captain has
agreed to take him as a passenger. Mathias looks through
the glass door at the little blue boat still being loaded in the
same laborious fashion.

"The captain is a friend of mine," the proprietor says. "He'll do it for you as a favor."

"Thank you very much. But I have my return ticket. It's still good—I don't want to waste it."

"They won't ask much, don't worry about that. Maybe the steamship line will refund your money anyway."

Mathias shrugs his shoulders. His eyes are following the silhouette of a man walking down the pier, coming from the landing slip.

"I don't think so," he says. "And I'd have to get on board right away, probably, wouldn't I?"

"You've still got a good quarter of an hour: plenty of time to get your things together."

"But not time to have lunch too."

"I can give you a quick cup of coffee."

The proprietor bends over the open cupboard to take out a cup, but Mathias stops him with a gesture of his hand and makes a face: "If I can't take my time over a good cup of *café au lait* with two or three rolls and butter, I'm not good for anything."

The proprietor lifts his arms and smiles, a sign that in that case he can do nothing more. Mathias turns his head toward the glass door. The fisherman in red clothes walking along the pier seems to have stayed in the same place while he was not looking; yet his regular pace must have brought him noticeably closer during these last remarks. It is easy to check his progress by means of the baskets and fishing tackle along the route. As Mathias watches him, the man quickly leaves these reference points behind, one after the other.

Mathias smiles back at the proprietor and adds: "Besides, I have to go and pay for my room. My landlady probably won't be home now."

A glance through the glass door affords him the same surprise: the fisherman is at exactly the same place he appeared to occupy a moment before, when Mathias' eyes had left him, still walking with the same even, rapid pace between the nets and traps. As soon as the observer stops watching him he stands still, continuing his movement at the very moment Mathias' eyes return to him—as if no interruption had occurred, for it is impossible to see him either start or stop.

"It's your business," the proprietor says. "If you want to stay with us so badly. . . . I'll bring you something right away."

"Thank you. I'm hungry this morning."

"I'm not surprised! You didn't eat anything last night."

"I'm usually hungry in the morning."

"In any case, nobody can say you don't like the country around here! You'd think you were afraid of missing a day of it."

"Oh, I know the country quite well—I've known it for a long time. Didn't I tell you I was born here?"

"You had plenty of time to drink a cup of coffee and get your things. As for the money, you'll spend more staying here."

"Well, that's too bad. I don't like making decisions at the last minute."

"It's your business. I'll bring you something right away. . . . Hey! Here's little Louis now."

The door opens to admit a sailor in a faded red uniform— the one who was walking on the pier just now. Besides, his face was not unfamiliar to Mathias.

"Don't bother," the proprietor says to him. "He doesn't want anything to do with your old tub."

The salesman smiles amiably at the young man: "I'm not in such a hurry as all that, you know," he says.

"I thought you wanted to leave the island right away," the proprietor says.

Mathias glances at him stealthily. The man seems to have meant nothing in particular by his remark. The young sailor, his hand still on the doorknob, looks at each of them in turn. His face is thin and severe. His eyes seem to see nothing.

"No," Mathias repeats, "I'm not in such a hurry."

No one answers. The proprietor, leaning in the doorway behind the bar, is facing the sailor wearing the red canvas jumper and trousers. The young man's eyes are turned toward the back wall, to the corner of the room occupied by the pin-ball machine. It looks as if he were waiting for someone.

He finally mutters three or four words—and goes out. The proprietor exits too—by the other door, into the room behind the bar—but returns almost at once. He walks around the bar to the glass door to look outside.

"This drizzle," he says, "will last all day."

He continues his commentary on the weather—the island's climate in general and the meteorological conditions during the last weeks. Although Mathias had feared another discussion of his poor reasons for not leaving, the man, on the contrary, seems to approve heartily of his decision: today is scarcely a good day, actually, to risk going out in a fishing boat. Not that there is much danger of seasickness in a calm like this, but on so modest a trawler there is nowhere to keep out of the spray; the salesman would be soaked to the skin before reaching port.

The proprietor also mentions the filthiness of such boats: no matter how much time is spent washing them down, there is always some fish refuse around, as if it grew there as fast as it could be cleaned away. And it is impossible to touch an inch of rope without covering your hands with grease.

Mathias glances at the man stealthily. Evidently he spoke without any special meaning—with no meaning at all—he

was merely talking for the sake of conversation, without
attaching the slightest importance to what he was saying,
without insistence or conviction; he might just as well be
saying nothing.

The young barmaid appears from the room behind the
bar, walking with tiny steps and carrying on a tray the silverware for breakfast. She sets it down on Mathias' table. She
knows where everything belongs now and no longer makes
the errors or the hesitations of the first day. An almost imperceptible deliberation still betrays her attention to her
work. When she has finished arranging the silverware, she
lifts her large, dark eyes to the traveler's face to see if he is
satisfied—but without waiting longer than a second, a flicker
of her eyelashes. It seems to him that she has smiled faintly
at him this time.

After a final, roundabout inspection of the table service,
she stretches out her arm as if to move something—the coffee-
pot, for instance—but everything is in order. Her hand is
small, the wrist almost too delicate. The cord had cut into
both wrists, making deep red lines. Yet she was not bound
very tightly. The cord must have sunk into the flesh because
of her futile efforts to get free. He had been forced to tie her
ankles too—not together, which would have been easy—but
separately, each one attached to the ground, about a yard
apart.

For this purpose, Mathias still had a good piece of string,
for it was longer than he had thought at first. In addition
he would need two stakes solidly planted in the ground. . . .
It was the sheep grazing nearby that furnished the ideal
solution to this problem. Why had he not thought of it before? First he ties her feet together, so that she will lie still
while he goes to shift the pickets; the sheep haven't time to
move before he has swiftly attached them all to a single peg
—instead of their original grouping into two pairs and one

solitary animal. He thus recovers two of the metal pegs—
pointed stakes with a loop at the top.

He had the most difficulty in restoring the sheep to their
respective tetherings, for they had taken fright in the mean-
time. They ran in terrified circles at the ends of the taut
cords. . . . She, on the other hand, was lying very still now,
her hands hidden under her, behind the small of her back
—her legs spread and slightly apart, her mouth swollen by
the gag.

Everything becomes even calmer: the chromium-plated
bicycle has been left in the hollow of the cliff, lying on the
slope, conspicuous against the background of short weeds.
Its contours are perfectly clear, with no suspicion of disorder
and no blurred areas, despite the complication of its parts.
The polished metal does not reflect the sun, doubtless because of the fine layer of dust from the road—almost a vapor
—deposited on it. Mathias calmly drinks the rest of the *café
au lait*.

The proprietor, who has again taken up his observation
post behind the glass door, announces the little trawler's
departure. The hull gradually slides away from the oblique
stone rim; between can be seen the widening streak of black
water.

"You could have been home by four o'clock," the proprietor says without turning around.

"Oh well, no one is expecting me," Mathias answers.

The other man says nothing, still watching the boat
maneuvering—it now turns so that it is headed in a line
perpendicular to its original direction, the stem facing the
entrance to the harbor. In spite of the distance, the letters
painted in white on the hull are still legible.

Mathias gets up from the table. One last reason—he adds—
keeps him on the island until tomorrow: before leaving, he
still would like to finish his rounds, which had remained

uncompleted the first night. Since he now had more time than he needed, he had done nothing the day before—or virtually nothing—relying on this third day to finish up the last part of his rounds at his usual rate. He explains to the proprietor the general plan of his itinerary: a kind of figure eight, of which the town constitutes not precisely the center, but a point along the side of one of the two loops—the northwest one. At the tip of this loop is Horses Point. It is the ground between Horses Point and the harbor—less than a quarter of his anticipated route—that he has to cover again, but thoroughly this time, without missing a single house or neglecting the least side road. In a hurry last Tuesday, he had actually abandoned most of the little groups of houses that were not on the main road. Finally he had had to go on without stopping at all, not even at doors he passed right before, traveling at the fastest speed the bicycle could manage.

Today he would not need to rent a bicycle for such a short route: there was plenty of time to do it on foot. Nevertheless, he prefers starting out right away and not coming back to town for lunch. So he wonders if the proprietor would make him two ham sandwiches—he would pick them up here in ten minutes, when he comes back with his suitcase—the one with the wrist watches.

The landlady catches sight of him from her open kitchen window when he steps into the hallway. She cries out a cheerful "Good morning, sir." He realizes at once that she has nothing particular to say to him—and nothing general either. Yet she steps over to the door; he himself stops; she asks him if he has slept well—yes; he didn't close his shutters last night—no; when the east wind blows, it's not a good idea to leave them open during the day . . . etc.

In his room he immediately notices the suitcase is not under the table. But then he remembers having put it elsewhere this morning. He opens the big cupboard—with his fingertips, since it has neither key nor handle—removes his suitcase, closes the cupboard again. This time he leaves the house by the door, and takes the main road to town. The raindrops have become so infrequent and so tiny that it requires particular attention to notice them at all.

Mathias enters the café "A l'Espérance," puts the sandwiches, which are wrapped in yellow paper, in the left pocket of his duffle coat, and continues toward the little square, walking on the cobbles washed clean by the rain, revealing all their colors.

The hardware shopwindow is empty: all the objects have been removed. Inside, a man in a gray jacket is standing on the display case, facing the street. His black felt slippers, his socks, and the bottoms of his trousers, raised by the movement of his arms, are exposed in broad daylight, about a yard above the ground. He is holding a big rag in each hand; the left hand is merely pressing against the glass, while the right is cleaning the surface with short, circular gestures.

As soon as he has walked around the shop corner, Mathias finds himself face to face with a young girl. He steps back to let her pass. But she stands where she is, staring at him as if she intended to speak to him, shifting her eyes several times from his suitcase to his face.

"Good morning, sir," she says at last. "Aren't you the watch salesman?"

It is Maria Leduc. She was just looking for Mathias; she was on the way to the house where he was staying, for she had heard he was still on the island. She wants to buy herself a watch—something sturdy.

Mathias decides it is no use to go back with her to her mother's house—the last house as you leave town on the road to the big lighthouse—which would take him out of his way now. He points to the sidewalk surrounding the monument: now that the rain has stopped, that would be a good place to look at his merchandise. He sets down the suitcase on the damp stones and opens the clasp.

While lifting out the first strips of cardboard, which he piles one by one in the cover after having shown them to his customer, he mentions the fact that he missed her at Black Rocks, hoping she will voluntarily make some allusion to the tragic accident that has taken her little sister from her. But the girl shows no intention of discussing the subject, and he will have to lead into it more directly. She cuts Mathias' polite formulas short, however, and confines herself to telling him the time of the funeral—Friday morning. Her words make it clear that the family prefers the simplest possible ceremony and the presence of only the closest relatives. It was as if they persisted in their bitterness toward the dead girl; she had no time to delay, she said, returning to the subject of the sale. In a few minutes she has made her choice and decided on the best way to conclude the transaction: the salesman is to leave the watch at the café where he takes his meals; for her part, she will leave the money there too. No sooner had Mathias closed his suitcase than Maria Leduc left.

On the other side of the monument he notices that the bulletin-board is covered with a completely white sheet of paper pasted on the surface of the wood. At this moment the garageman comes out of his tobacco shop carrying a little bottle and a fine brush. Mathias asks him what happened to the sign that was up the day before: it wasn't the right one, the garageman answers, for the film they had sent along with it; the distributor had made an error in the shipment. He would have to announce next Sunday's program by a hand-made ink inscription. Mathias leaves the man already busy with his task, firmly tracing a large letter O.

After taking the street to the left of the town hall, the

salesman passes the end of the old harbor, completely empty at low tide—for the tide-gate there has not held in the water for years. Here too the mud has evidently been raked.

Next he follows the high wall of the fort. The road beyond returns to the coast, but without sloping down to the shore itself, and continues curving left, toward the point.

Mathias reaches the fork leading to the village of Saint-Sauveur much sooner than he expected—this was the last point he had systematically canvassed. He sold only one watch here—the last of the day—but since he has visited the principal residences, zealously and not over-hastily, it is futile to try his chances here once again.

Hence he sets out on the main road itself in the opposite direction, walking rapidly toward town.

After about fifty yards he comes upon an isolated cottage on his right, built at the edge of the road—which he had not bothered with on Tuesday because of its poverty-stricken aspect. Nevertheless, it is much like the other buildings on the island: a simple ground floor with two small square windows on each side of a low door.

He knocks on the door panel and waits, holding his suitcase in his left hand. The shiny finish, freshly repainted, imitates with remarkable accuracy the veins and irregularities of wood. At eye level are two round knots drawn side by side, so that they look like a pair of glasses. The salesman knocks again, this time with his ring.

He hears steps in the hallway. The door opens on a woman's head—with no expression whatever—neither welcoming nor scowling, neither confident nor mistrustful, not even surprised.

"Good morning, madame," he says. "Would you like to look at some splendid watches unlike any you've ever seen before, of ideal manufacture, guaranteed unbreakable, shockproof, waterproof, and at prices that will surprise you? Just take a look at them! You'll never regret the time—only a moment; it doesn't commit you to a thing. Just take a look!"

"All right," the woman says. "Come in."

He makes his way down the hallway, then through the first door on the right into the kitchen. He sets down his suitcase on the big oval table in the middle of the room. The new oilcloth is decorated with a pattern of small many-colored flowers.

He opens the clasp by pressing on it with his fingertips. He seizes the cover in both hands—one on each side, thumbs over the reinforced corners with the copper rivets—and folds it back. The cover remains wide open, its outer edge resting on the oilcloth. The salesman takes the black memorandum book out of the suitcase with his right hand and puts it in the cover. Then he picks up the prospectuses and puts them on top of the memorandum book.

With his left hand he then takes hold of the first rectangular strip of cardboard by its lower left corner and holds it at the level of his chest, tilted at an angle of forty-five degrees, the two long sides parallel to the table top. Between the thumb and index finger of his right hand he takes hold of the protecting paper attached to the upper part of the cardboard strip; holding this paper by its lower right corner, he raises it, making it pivot on its hinge until it has made a rotation of more than one hundred eighty degrees. Then he lets go of this paper which, still fastened to the cardboard strip by one edge, continues its rotating movement until it occupies once again a vertical position next to the cardboard strip, although slightly askew because of the natural stiffness of the leaf. Meanwhile the right hand returns toward the salesman's chest, that is, lowered to the level of the center of the cardboard strip, while moving toward the left. The thumb and index finger are extended forward, pressed together, while the other three fingers curve toward the interior of the palm. The end of the extended finger approaches the circle formed by the face of the watch attached to . . .

. . . circle formed by the face of the watch attached to his wrist and said: "Four-fifteen, exactly."

At the base of the glass, he saw his long, pointed fingernail. Of course the salesman did not file them to look like that. And tonight, as soon as . . .

"It's on time, today," the woman said.

She walked away toward the bow of the little steamer, immediately swallowed up by the crowd of passengers on deck. Most of them had not yet taken their seats for the crossing; they were wandering aimlessly about the deck, looking for comfortable places to sit, bumping into one another, calling directions, piling and counting luggage; others were standing along the railing next to the pier, waving a last farewell to those remaining behind.

Mathias also leaned on the gunwale and stared at the water; a wave had just broken against the stone slope. The lapping undulations of the surface, in the sheltered angle of the landing slip, were weak but regular. Farther to the right, the ridge formed by the inclined plane and the vertical embankment began its oblique retreating movement.

The whistle blew a last shrill, prolonged blast. The gangway's electric bell sounded. Against the ship's hull the darker strip of water widened almost imperceptibly.

On the pier, beneath the thin sheet of liquid covering the stone, the slightest unevenness of the blocks could be clearly distinguished, as well as the joints in the cement separating them by more or less hollow lines. The relief was both more apparent than it would have been in air, and more unreal, made noticeable by shadows that were emphasized—exaggerated, perhaps—without quite giving the impression of real outcroppings: as if they had been painted in *trompe-l'oeil*.

The tide was still rising, although it was already high compared to its level this morning, when the steamer arrived. The salesman was standing at the gangway watching the passengers: there were only civilians with benign faces, local people returning home to be met on the pier by their wives and children.

At the bottom of the portion of the inclined plane that was still dry, a slightly stronger wave suddenly wet a new area, less than six inches wide. When it retreated, a number of gray and yellow marks, previously invisible, appeared on the granite.

The water in the sheltered angle rose and fell, reminding the salesman of the swell several miles offshore as it ran against a floating buoy the ship had passed. It occurred to him that in about three hours he would be on land. He stepped back a little, in order to glance at the fiber suitcase at his feet.

It was a heavy iron buoy, the portion above water constituting a cone surmounted by a complex assemblage of metal stems and plates. The structure extended three or four yards into the air. The conical support itself represented nearly half of this height. The rest was divided into three noticeably similar parts: first, prolonging the point of the cone, a narrow, openwork, square turret—four iron uprights connected by crosspieces; above this came a kind of cylindrical cage, its vertical bars sheltering a signal light fastened in the middle; and last, topping the structure and separated from the cylinder by a stem which continued its main axis, three equilateral triangles, superimposed so that the tip of one supported in its center the horizontal base of the next. The whole of this structure was painted a shiny black.

Since the buoy was not light enough to follow the movement of the waves, the water level rose and fell according